THE FORTUNES OF TEXAS

*Follow the lives and loves of a complex family
with a rich history and deep ties
in the Lone Star State*

HITTING THE JACKPOT

The Maloneys of Chatelaine, Texas,
have just discovered they are blood relations
to the Fortunes—which makes them instant
millionaires. But their inheritance comes
with a big secret attached that could change
everything for their small-town family...

Now that he's going to be rich, bartender
Damon Fortune Maloney can't wait to live
his best single life. So why is the fun-loving
bachelor so drawn to Sari Keeling? The
gorgeous widowed mom of two is convinced
Damon is her Mr. Wrong, but Damon knows that
some rules are meant to be broken...

Dear Reader,

I can't tell you how excited I was to be invited to write my first Fortunes of Texas romance for Harlequin Special Edition. This long-standing series is one I have enjoyed for years. While writing *Fortune's Fatherhood Dare*, I fell in love with this couple and Sari's adorable two- and four-year-old little boys. I flipped through old photo albums and thought back to a time when my grown sons were this age and then used some of my favorite memories to bring these characters to life. I hope they make you smile as much as I did while writing.

Damon Fortune Maloney is expecting a large inheritance and plans to enjoy dating life once he gets his money, but when he meets widowed single mom Sari Keeling and boasts he can handle any kid, she dares him to take care of her two toddlers. When a day of babysitting turns into family dinners and outings, he realizes parenthood is tougher than he thought, and so is resisting Sari.

I hope you enjoy *Fortune's Fatherhood Dare*. As always, thank you for reading!

Best wishes,

Makenna Lee

Fortune's Fatherhood Dare

MAKENNA LEE

HARLEQUIN
SPECIAL
EDITION

Special thanks and acknowledgment are given to
Makenna Lee for her contribution to
The Fortunes of Texas: Hitting the Jackpot miniseries.

HARLEQUIN®
SPECIAL EDITION™

Recycling programs
for this product may
not exist in your area.

ISBN-13: 978-1-335-72455-7

Fortune's Fatherhood Dare

Copyright © 2023 by Harlequin Enterprises ULC

For questions and comments about the quality of this book,
please contact us at CustomerService@Harlequin.com.

Harlequin Enterprises ULC
22 Adelaide St. West, 41st Floor
Toronto, Ontario M5H 4E3, Canada
www.Harlequin.com

Printed in U.S.A.

Makenna Lee is an award-winning romance author living in the Texas Hill Country with her real-life hero and their two children, one of whom has Down syndrome and inspired her first Harlequin book, *A Sheriff's Star*. She writes heartwarming contemporary romance that celebrates real-life challenges and the power of love and acceptance. She has been known to make people laugh and cry in the same book. Makenna is often drinking coffee with a cat on her lap while writing, reading or plotting a new story. Her wish is to write stories that touch your heart, making you feel, think and dream.

Books by Makenna Lee

Harlequin Special Edition

Home to Oak Hollow

A Sheriff's Star
In the Key of Family
A Child's Christmas Wish
A Marriage of Benefits
Lessons in Fatherhood
The Bookstore's Secret

The Fortunes of Texas: Hitting the Jackpot

Fortune's Fatherhood Dare

Visit the Author Profile page
at Harlequin.com for more titles.

To my husband, Brian.
My fortune is having a family with you! XOXO

Chapter One

The Chatelaine Report: Money must be a great aphrodisiac, as three of the Fortune Maloney brothers have found love since the beginning of the year. There's only one left, but we defy anyone to tie Damon Fortune Maloney down. (Though many would like to!) Everyone's favorite bartender has promised that even after he is wealthy, he has no intention of abandoning the single life. We wonder what it would take to tempt Damon down the aisle...

The day Damon Fortune Maloney left his old, smoking truck on the side of the road and walked into town is the day he used his good credit score and his

name—the one that made people think of money—
and financed a luxury convertible.

With the surround sound playing the latest num-
ber- one country song, he inhaled the rich scent of
leather. The buttery soft upholstery covered bucket
seats equipped with built-in heat, AC and massage
options. The monthly payments were eye-popping
to say the least, but he had a plan. Kind of. His sister
and three older brothers had received their share of
Wendell Fortune's estate a few months apart, and he
was next in line to inherit from a grandfather none
of them had ever known.

Damon pressed the gas pedal and merged smoothly
into highway traffic, the V-8 engine purring beneath
him like a well-satisfied woman. And satisfaction
was something every woman deserved. It was one
of his top rules.

Several heads turned as he pulled into a parking
spot at the Chatelaine Bar and Grill a few minutes
before his shift. There would be questions about his
new car and the assumption that he'd received his
inheritance, which he had not.

It will come soon. It has to.

He couldn't let himself think otherwise. Until then,
he would put off his home renovation projects, and if
necessary, he'd pick up an extra bartending shift each
week. Rather than tossing his sunglasses on the dash
like he'd done with the drugstore pair, he stored his
new designer shades in their case. He stuffed a few

peppermints into the front pocket of his black jeans and got out of his new silver baby. It locked with a very satisfying chirp of the alarm, something his truck never had. He waved to several regular customers who had paused their conversation to gawk at him. He didn't stop to field questions about his new car. It was Tuesday, and he was never late on ladies' night.

As he neared the front door, a little boy of about six ran over to him with his chocolate Lab on a red leash. He recognized the kid from the T-ball team he'd helped coach. "Hey there, Johnny."

"Mr. Damon, you got candy today?"

"You know it, kiddo." He tossed a peppermint to the child, scratched the dog behind the ears and then waved to the boy's parents, who were whispering as they stared at him.

Turning the heads of most women was something Damon had grown accustomed to, but he didn't usually draw the attention of every man, woman, child *and* dog. The attention was no doubt because of the shiny silver car and his new ostrich-leather cowboy boots. And in the case of the little boy, it was possibly his pocket full of candy. He'd never needed the fancy accessories to get attention from the female population. The car and sunglasses and boots were just whipped topping.

Chatelaine Bar and Grill was painted across one side of the two-story wooden building. The vertical boards were weathered, and the roof was tin, fitting the mining theme of the restaurant. Damon opened the heavy timber door that led into a waiting area with benches. It was decorated with framed photographs and other props paying homage to Chatelaine's mining past.

In the dining room, red leather banquette seating stretched along two walls, some of them tucked into alcoves with mood lighting. There were sturdy wooden tables and chairs in the center and along the back wall of windows that looked out over the patio and the natural area beyond. A couple of firepits, scattered seating and a few outdoor games made the patio a fun hangout place.

Damon clocked in, put on the extra white button-up from his locker and made his way to the bar that was off to one side near the back of the restaurant. It was a masculine, antique wooden bar that had once been in a saloon.

Like clockwork, the Silver Ladies—a group of elderly women who had a walking club—arrived with their usual enthusiasm. After a bit of harmless flirtation, they would order their usual one glass of wine and salads before going home to watch their "shows."

"Hello, lovely ladies. How are all of you this evening?"

"It's Silver Ladies," the petite one with lots of jewelry said, and smoothed her gray hair as if to point out the reason for the name.

"My mistake. You should add lovely to the name," he said, mirroring her smile.

"Look at you, young charmer, making Marybelle titter like a schoolgirl," said the tallest of the group, but she looked equally thrilled by his suggestion.

He loved making them smile and giggle. In his book, no woman was ever too old for flattery. After filling their drink order, he poured beers for Alec Ramsey and Paul Scott, who had picked out a center table to wait for the rest of the GreatStore employees who were meeting up tonight. Damon had never worked at the one-stop-shop store where you could buy everything from groceries to new tires, but a good portion of the town's younger residents had worked there at one time or another.

Damon waved to his brothers Lincoln and Cooper as they neared the bar. So much had changed for them lately. Linc was the oldest and most serious of the four brothers, and it wasn't all that surprising that he was engaged to Remi, a wonderful woman who seemed to be just what his brother needed. But shockingly, Cooper, the wild child of the family, was engaged, and Alana was expecting a baby.

All three of his brothers had settled down, but Damon was definitely not following them down that path. At least not yet. He had big plans to live up the single life, especially once he was a wealthy man.

"Where are your better halves?" he asked, referring to Remi and Alana.

"They'll be here in a minute," Linc said. "I'll have the usual, and Remi wants red wine."

Cooper shifted his cowboy hat. "Alana wants a sparkling water with mint and lemon. She's been having some interesting pregnancy cravings."

"I can do that. Is Max coming Tonight?" Damon asked about their other brother.

"No," Linc said. "Eliza has a real estate event they had to attend."

Damon grabbed a mug, filled it with the Rising Fortune's IPA on tap and then handed it to Linc. He stuck a second mug under the Shiner Bock tap just as Remi and Alana came inside, and they weren't alone. The strikingly gorgeous woman between them was no one he'd ever seen. He would've remembered this goddess with her long, wavy red hair and crystal blue eyes he could happily get lost in. His surroundings blurred, except for the music, and he wasn't entirely sure if it was playing on the sound system or in his head.

Damon jolted when foamy beer overflowed the mug. A cold wet hand and his brothers' snorts of laughter jerked him the rest of the way out of his fantasy. *Well, hell.* He yanked the bar towel from his waistband.

"Head in the game, bartender," Coop said. "I'm not paying for that beer you're spilling."

Linc took a sip of his perfectly poured IPA. "Coop, you could buy the whole keg and not even notice."

Damon ignored his siblings and stole a few more glances at the beauty while cleaning up spilled beer.

"Speaking of buying things… Setting up a room for the baby is majorly expensive. Do you have any idea how much stuff one baby needs?" Coop asked, as if their oldest brother hadn't pointed out the fact that he was now a millionaire.

"No idea." Damon set a fresh mug of beer in front of Coop and started on drinks for the women. Obviously, his brothers had not heard about his new car, because if they had, he would've gotten the third degree straight away. But in this small town, it was only a matter of time before everyone knew. His defense? It was hard watching his three older brothers and his sister living in comfort and wealth while he still had to scrimp and scrape to make ends meet after paying the mortgage on his 1970s fixer-upper. This wasn't the place where he wanted to get into the fact that he'd spent money he didn't have yet.

"Who is the woman sitting between Remi and Alana?" he asked.

Coop chuckled. "So, that's who you were gawking at. That's Sari Keeling. She works with Alana at GreatStore, and they have become friends."

As if Sari had heard them talking about her, she looked straight at Damon. Her lips parted slightly, and her eyes widened before she quickly ducked her head. He could take her reaction in a couple of ways. One, she was shy. Two, she didn't return his interest.

Her eyes flickered his way once again, briefly, but he'd caught it. He decided to go with the shy version and see where it took them.

"Sari seems nice," Linc said, and grabbed Remi's wine. "You should come over and say hello to her."

His brothers took their drinks and headed back to the table of friends. Damon liked his job, but missing out on happy hour with friends was a drawback. He served more beer, a few mixed drinks and a scotch on the rocks, then looked around and saw that everyone had a drink, except for the woman he needed to meet. A minute later, Sari headed his way.

Some of her auburn hair fell over one shoulder, trailing almost down to her waist. He imagined what it would be like to run his fingers through the wavy strands and heat washed over him. "Welcome to the Chatelaine, Sari. I'm Damon."

Her head cocked to the side. "How do you know my name?"

"Special bartender powers."

She glanced over her shoulder to the table of friends before turning back to him with a smile. "I guess you know everyone over there?"

"I do. Linc and Coop are my brothers. What can I get for you?" He definitely wouldn't mind getting Sari's phone number and a date. And once he was wealthy like his siblings, he'd love to wine and dine and spoil this woman in style.

Sari spread her hands on the dark wood bar top as

if it were grounding her. Her fingers were long and elegant with no rings and cotton-candy-pink polish on her nails. How would they feel scraping lightly over the skin on his back? He shivered at the idea of it.

"I guess…" She drummed her fingers while looking at the bottles lined up behind him on the shelves. "A white wine."

"You don't sound very convinced." He chuckled and leaned his forearms on the bar top, putting them a few inches closer together. Close enough to catch the scent of peaches. "I can mix a special cocktail just for you. Do you like strawberries or raspberries?"

"Raspberries. They are sweet but also tart on your tongue."

Just hearing her talk about something being on her tongue made his mouth water. "Good choice. Are you okay with rum?"

"Yes, but no tequila." She shuddered and got that look on her face that told him she'd once overindulged on that particular liquor.

"Got it. Do you trust me?"

She studied him while worrying her bottom lip with her teeth. "Hmm. I'm not usually much of a gambler, but since it's a rare night out for me, I'll go for it."

"If you don't like the drink, I'll make something else or pour you that glass of white wine, because I never let a woman leave unsatisfied."

Sari pressed her lips together and her eyes scanned what she could see of him. "Is that so?"

"It's one of my top rules."

"What are your other rules?" she asked, and took a seat on one of the barstools.

He was happy to see she wasn't in a rush to get away from him. "Oh, I can't tell you yet. I have to really know someone before I reveal all of them." She was coming out of the shyness he'd first sensed, and he liked it. He dropped fresh raspberries and a couple of lime wedges into a shaker.

With her elbows on the bar, she propped her chin on her clasped hands, watching him intently as if she'd be expected to make the next drink. "We've only just met, and I already know two of them. You like to satisfy women, and you don't share all of your rules at once."

"It must be a sign." Damon added sugar to the fruit and muddled them together.

"A sign of what?"

"For one, that you are very observant, and that we should spend some time together so you can discover the rest."

"What do you call this drink?"

"I haven't decided. It's like a raspberry version of a mojito. Maybe you can help me name it after you taste it."

"Maybe I will."

He added a few mint leaves and white rum, gave the mixture a shake, and then topped it off with sparkling water. "Have you been in here before?"

"It's my first time."

"Firsts can be the start of something good." What firsts could they discover together?

"Only good?" she asked in an innocent voice, but her eyes sparked with playfulness.

I think I could love this woman.

"Possibly mind-blowing." He stuck a bright yellow straw in her drink. "Time for the test. And it's on the house since you will help me name it."

With her pretty pink glossy lips wrapped around the straw, she sipped and made a satisfied sound. "Mmm. It's delicious."

A customer stepped up to the bar before he could figure out a way to tell her he'd like the opportunity to show her how delicious they could be together. "Don't go anywhere. I'll be right back."

What rotten timing to have the other bartender running late and one waitress out sick. While mixing a margarita, he watched Alana give Sari a thumbs-up and then they did some kind of coded hand signs that he couldn't make sense off, but they seemed to be entertained by their silent conversation. To his delight, Sari did wait while he served several customers. Once he got back to her, half of her drink was gone.

"So, have you thought of a good name?"

She licked her lips. "I'm thinking… Berry Delish."

"Hey, Damon. Can I have a set of darts?" a young man asked.

"Sure thing. Just bring them back when you're done." He reached under the bar and grabbed the red and blue set.

Sari turned to see where the guy went. "There are dartboards here?"

"Three of them. You play?"

"I haven't in a while, but I used to be pretty good."

When he played, he almost always won. "I have a break in a while. Want to play a game?"

"That sounds fun, but right now, I should stop monopolizing your time." She stood and picked up her cocktail. "Let me know when you go on your break."

"You got it."

While he worked, Damon was having a hell of a time concentrating and made a couple of drinks wrong, but sharing several smiles with Sari made it worth the extra work. When the second bartender finally arrived, Damon told him he was taking a longer break than usual.

He motioned to Sari in a way that asked if she wanted a second drink, and she nodded. He mixed it, grabbed the darts and was glad when Sari got up to come over to him. If he went over to the table, that would waste too much time talking to the group, and he wanted to spend every minute of his break getting to know her.

"Thank you," she said as she drew close and took the glass from him.

Damon stopped in front of the dartboards that

were tucked around a corner, so there was no chance of stray darts accidentally flying toward customers having dinner. "You work at GreatStore?"

"Yes. Since February."

"Where did you live and work before that?"

"In San Antonio. I worked at a grocery store and then a pet store. I get around," she said with a smile.

He set the darts on a tall pub table. "Do you get bored easily and need a change?"

"No. I need flexible hours, and employers aren't always flexible. So I've had to change jobs more frequently than I'd like."

"You should bartend here with me. I'd love to train you." A pretty pink flush bloomed on her cheeks and her soft laugh made his skin tingle.

"I'm not a night owl, and I'll probably be ready to go home by eight o'clock."

Damon looked at his watch. "That's a real shame. All the best stuff happens after dark."

"Not in my house." She hitched both of her thumbs toward her own chest. "Single mom with two toddlers. Ages two and four."

Damon's eyebrows arched at two different angles. "Really? I almost carded you because you barely look old enough to drink."

"I'm definitely old enough for a lot of things."

He liked the sound of that and wouldn't mind exploring the topic a bit more. "I'm twenty-seven, and you must be younger than me."

Sari smiled while sipping her drink. "Thanks for the compliment, but I'm old enough that I could have been your...babysitter. I'm thirty-two."

"No way." He would have loved having her for a babysitter. He had appreciated the beauty of women for as long as he could remember. Neither her age nor the fact that she had children was a deterrent. "I'm great with kids."

"Oh, really?"

"Probably because I'm a big kid myself. I've never met a kid I couldn't babysit."

With her head tilted, she studied him for a moment. "I dare you to babysit my kids."

Chapter Two

Sari Keeling couldn't believe she was flirting with the guy who had caught her attention at the Valentine's Bachelor Auction. The really handsome one she had thought about more than once over the weeks since then. Up close, Damon was even more appealing and gave off a sexy vibe that made her tingle with sensations she hadn't felt in quite some time. He hadn't seemed shocked at her dare to babysit, but no doubt his senses would kick in at any moment.

Damon held up a purple dart. "Want to make a friendly wager?"

Or he'll just change the subject. "What do you have in mind? Something other than money?"

"If I win the game of darts, you agree to go out to dinner with me one night soon." He rolled the dart between the pads of his thumb and pointer finger. "And if you win…you get a free night of babysitting."

Surprise, surprise. Maybe he's braver than I thought.

"Deal." She held out her hand, and when they shook, a tingle spiraled through her body, followed by a shiver that she knew he'd felt, too.

His white dress shirt was unbuttoned just enough to reveal a black T-shirt beneath, hinting at the bad boy she thought he might be. One she probably should not be getting mixed up with. Damon wouldn't know what to do with someone like her. Her life came with a list of responsibilities and challenges that would likely make his head explode.

"Want to be the green or purple darts?" Damon asked.

"Purple, please. It's my two-year-old's favorite color."

"You throw first," Damon said, and put three darts on her open palm.

The brush of his fingers against her skin made her want to shiver again, but she tensed her muscles. "Get ready to lose."

"Trash talk. I like it."

She got into the throwing stance her cousin had taught her, wiggled her hips into the correct position and let the dart fly. It landed just right of the bull's-eye.

"Not bad," he said. "Do you have boys or girls or one of each?"

"Two boys." She glanced at him over her shoulder. "Are you trying to distract me?"

"Never." His crooked grin told an entirely different story.

What would've happened if she had bid on him at the bachelor auction and they'd gone out on a real date? She remembered reading in the auction program what he'd offered. A sunset dinner cruise on Lake Chatelaine. An evening that sounded very romantic. She almost laughed aloud when she remembered the woman who had won him was in the range of eighty to ninety years old. His smile had never faltered as he'd taken her by the arm and guided her back to her table. This bad boy seemed to have a lot of heart.

There could never be anything serious between her and Damon. He was too young and unencumbered and wouldn't understand her level of responsibility, but he sure was fun to hang out with. And to think she almost hadn't come out tonight. But when her neighbor, Mrs. Mata, offered to watch the boys for the evening, she hadn't been able to resist.

Sari threw another dart, landing on the other side of the bull's-eye. She wasn't doing too bad for not playing in forever.

"Where are your kids tonight? With their dad?"

A flash of pain threatened to derail her good

mood, but she'd become good at hiding it. "No. My next-door neighbor is watching them. This is a rare night out for me." So she intended to enjoy her time while she could.

"Young ladies like you should get out more than rarely."

"You think so?" Proof he didn't understand a single mother's world, and their flirting could not be taken seriously. It was flattering that Damon thought she was so young, but she felt years older than thirty-two. Life had delivered a series of curveballs and seen to aging her emotionally beyond her years, and she'd bet she had life experiences and challenges he had not. Damon was around the same age her husband had been when they'd married. But she and Seth had been at the same stage of life with plans to take each step and meet every challenge together.

She knew better than anyone…plans could change in a heartbeat.

A familiar but unwelcome heaviness tried to settle in her limbs, but she resisted the pull. She and Seth had had a beautiful life together, until it ended five years after their wedding. But she didn't want to share any of the details with Damon. It always brought down the mood, and she really didn't need any more pitying glances.

She threw her third dart and it hit home, square in the center. She heard his surprised oath before she turned with her arms raised high and did a celebratory shimmy dance, then retrieved her darts. "Your turn."

"I better be on my game tonight." He grabbed his darts, his arm brushing hers as he moved by, leaving the scent of leather and spices to tickle her nose.

Damon did well but not as well as she had. They were neck and neck, their points shifting back and forth between them, much like their flirty banter.

When she threw her final dart, it was a dead-on bull's-eye, making her the winner. She gave a little hop and cheer, then turned to see the shocked expression on his handsome face.

"I can't believe it," he said, and rested both arms on the tall pub table. "I haven't lost at darts in a long time. And you only said you were 'pretty good.' Was that luck, or are you an undercover professional dart player?"

She took a sip of her delicious fruity cocktail. "I'm no pro. And don't worry about the bet. I won't hold you to babysitting. The look of surprise on your face was more than enough satisfaction." She reached across the small round tabletop to pat his forearm. Damon covered her hand with his, and warmth radiated up her arm. She told herself to pull away, but she couldn't make herself break the contact. It was a connection she'd been craving and not even known it.

"And if I remember correctly, you did say something about women and satisfaction."

He chuckled. "I did say that, and I meant it. And I won't back out of our bet."

She forced herself to slide her hand out from under his and bit the inside of her cheek, suddenly unsure about the bet she'd made without giving it any real thought. Two drinks had gone to her head, and it was a good thing she wasn't driving tonight. "Now that I think about this wager, I don't know if babysitting is a good idea."

"How hard can it be to watch two little boys? I grew up with three brothers and a younger sister. You can't scare me."

Sari paused and looked him up and down from his head of dark brown wavy hair and moody brown eyes, along his lean muscular body to his fancy cowboy boots. "You haven't met *my* kids. They might tie you up with jump ropes and make you watch the same episode of *PAW Patrol* over and over. And over," she said in an exaggerated tone.

"I've never met a kid I couldn't win over," he said confidently.

Or a woman, I'd bet.

Sari suddenly snapped into the reality of her life with a prickle of goose bumps. What was she thinking? She couldn't let a guy she'd just met babysit her boys. Benjy and Jacob were her life. Her everything.

Damon shifted a bit closer. "I can see the worry on your face, and I understand your concern. You don't really know me." He flashed another of his gorgeous lopsided grins. "Yet."

Something tingled deep inside her. Did he truly want to get to know her?

"You should get references," he suggested.

Glad that he understood her concern, she relaxed just a bit and picked up her drink. "And they will no doubt tell me that you are a fantastic guy?"

"Let's find out." He took hold of her free hand and led her over to the table of friends.

The warmth of his hand felt good. She should be surprised or uncomfortable about the contact, but she wasn't. How could it feel this natural to already be holding his hand?

"I have an announcement." He raised their joined hands, presenting her as champion after one game of darts. "Sari has beaten me at darts."

Some of them laughed and others cheered for her. She liked that he wasn't too cocky to admit he'd been beaten. Damon was fun and easygoing and had a magnetism that drew her in. She liked him way more than was smart, but how was she supposed to control this burst of attraction sparkling between them?

He lowered their hands, but he did not let go. "And now, I need references before I can pay my debt and babysit her kids. Who's got something good to say?" Damon asked the group.

"Well…" His brother Cooper feigned difficulty thinking of anything nice. "He's not a criminal."

Damon groaned. "I should have known y'all wouldn't be any help."

"He can watch my kids," Linc said.

His fiancée, Remi, shook her head. "You don't have any kids."

Linc just grinned and kissed her.

"I plan on letting him watch our baby," Alana said and spread both hands on her pregnant belly.

Sari turned her face to Damon. "Does it scare you to think about taking care of a baby?"

"Nope. As long as I'm not expected to wear that trippy male breastfeeding contraption we saw in that video." Damon gave a little squeeze before letting go of her hand. "I have to get back behind the bar. Everyone behave so I don't have to toss you out."

Sari was so tempted to watch him walk toward the bar but forced herself to focus on the people at the table as she took her seat between Remi and Alana.

Remi ran her fingers through her dark hair. "Girl, it didn't take you but a second to catch the eye of one of the hottest bachelors in town."

"Hey," Linc said to his fiancée. "Don't be saying my brother is hot right in front of me."

Remi rolled her eyes. "I meant like in high demand."

Linc's eyes narrowed as he rubbed his jawline. "I *guess* that's true."

"But he is hot," Remi said in a fake whisper that made Linc grimace.

Sari had worried about being a stranger in her new small town and having no friends in Chatelaine, but she really liked this group and was glad they'd talked her into coming out with them tonight.

When it came time for Alana to drive her home, Sari went up to the bar to say good-night to Damon. "Thanks again for the drinks and the game."

"You bet. I enjoyed our time together. Since I usually work nights, how about I babysit on a Saturday during the daytime? You can have a girls' day out or something." He pulled his cell phone from his back pocket, opened his contacts and handed it to her. "I need your number so we can finalize our plans."

"Did you lose the bet just to get my number?" she asked while typing it in.

"Pretty slick way to get it, right?"

She laughed and handed his phone back. "If you say so."

He touched his phone's screen and hers rang in her purse. "And now you have my number. I'll call you to set up details about babysitting."

"That works. Have a good night." Sari waved, and when she turned to go, a man stepped into her path.

"I'm gonna buy you a drink." He swayed unsteadily into her personal space.

She wrinkled her nose against the reek of alcohol, garlic and sweat. An unpleasant feeling snaked along her spine. "No thank you." When the man stumbled forward again and reached out to touch her, she stepped back even more, bumping into a barstool.

Damon was suddenly between them, and she hadn't even seen him come out from behind the bar. "Time to go home, Bud. I'll call you a cab."

The man swayed to the side. "Don't need a cab. My brother drove."

Damon made eye contact with another man who was walking toward them.

"Sorry. I'll get him out of here." He put an arm around his inebriated brother's shoulders and steered him away.

Damon reached forward as if to touch her but instead put his hand in his pocket as though reminding himself that touching her right after stopping a groping drunk guy from doing the same was not a wise decision. "Are you okay, Sari?"

"I'm fine. I've handled worse than him, but thanks for the assistance."

"I didn't serve him enough to be that drunk. Guess he came in already halfway there."

Alana called her name from the table and said they'd be outside.

"I better go," Sari said. "See you soon."

"You bet you will. Good night." He moved to go but paused and turned back. "Let me walk you to the door, just in case anyone else is misbehaving."

She started to argue that she was not the one who needed a babysitter, but in her book, chivalry should never be discouraged. And it felt kind of nice to once in a while be looked after. "Thank you."

He placed a hand lightly on her upper back to steer her through the dining room to the front door and out onto the sidewalk. "Good night, Sari."

She took a few steps backward to let him—and herself—know that even though it was tempting as hell, any more physical contact would only tempt her to lean in for a kiss. "Good night." She smiled once more, then turned for the car.

"You won't have to fight off guys like him if I'm around."

She wasn't sure if he'd meant for her to hear his statement or not. Was he trying to be her knight in shining armor? Was he really that kind of guy? She always told people she didn't need a protector, and she didn't.

But it might be nice to once in a while have someone to watch her back.

Sitting behind Cooper in the back seat of Alana's car, Sari's thoughts kept drifting back to Damon and the way he laughed easily. The way his quick smile reached his eyes. And the way he had sensed her uncertainty about babysitting her precious boys. If she was going to see him again—and that was highly likely since Chatelaine was a small town—she had to decide now what she was willing to let happen between them. Even after only the small amount of time they'd spent together, she knew remaining strictly friends with a man like Damon was going to be a tall order. Just like he was. Tall and very nicely sculpted, but not too bulky like he spent every day in the gym.

She would make it clear that she was not looking for a romance or a relationship. Not being on the same page had the potential to make things very awkward, and Sari hated it when things became awkward. It made her uncomfortable, made her want to stay in her house and avoid the situation. Being a busy single mom, she did not have the luxury of staying home whenever she wanted.

Keeping Damon in the friends-who-flirt zone was the safest, smartest option, but not nearly as appealing as one that involved touching him in ways friends normally did not. It had to be the alcohol that was making her act like she was in high school, because it wasn't like her to have such an instant crush. Was Damon the best option to be the first person she dated since Seth?

In the front seat, Alana and Cooper were discussing some of the houses and properties they were considering buying.

In a tender gesture, Cooper reached across the space between them and brushed his fingers through Alana's long blonde hair. "I think we should go with the ranch that has the little guest house. It's the perfect size to turn into your photography studio.".

"I really do like that one," Alana said.

Sari leaned toward them. "That sounds like the perfect thing for you. You know the boys and I will be your first customers. And speaking of my boys, is Damon really responsible enough to take care of my kids for a few hours?"

Cooper chuckled and then shifted in the front passenger seat so he could see her in the back. "He's my little brother and I tease him, but he is responsible and won't let anything happen to your kids. He's good with our sister's son."

"You don't need to worry." Alana put on the blinker before turning into the parking lot of Sari's small apartment complex. "Coop is right."

That made Sari feel a little better about the whole babysitting thing.

Alana put the car in Park and turned to look at Sari. "My baby bump is to the point where I'm having trouble getting to my feet, and I need a pedicure. Want to go do that with me on Saturday? My treat."

"I haven't had a pedicure for ages. And since I suddenly find myself with a babysitter, that sounds perfect."

"Oh, good. Call me tomorrow and we can figure out a time," Alana said.

Sari opened the car door. "I will. Thanks for the ride."

She waved as they drove away, then walked across the center courtyard of her small U-shaped apartment complex of twelve units. As she unlocked her door, she could hear the TV softly playing.

Mrs. Mata, a former elementary school teacher, turned off her movie. "Did you have fun tonight?"

"I did. How'd the boys behave for you?"

"We did just fine." She got up from Sari's over-stuffed red chair, her silver-streaked black hair falling in a sleek bob to her shoulders. "Only one episode of their cartoon and a mild fight over the last granola bar, but we got it worked out quickly by splitting it in two."

"I really appreciate you watching them tonight."

"I'm happy to help. I know what it's like to be a single mom." Mrs. Mata picked up her keys from the coffee table. "Playing with them helps keep me young."

"Well, I'm happy to share them anytime you want." Once Sari had locked the door behind her neighbor, she went down the hallway to look in on her boys. They were sound asleep. With a thumb in his mouth, Jacob was on his tummy with his knees tucked up under him and his little bottom in the air. Benjy was sprawled out like a starfish with his feet on the pillow. She tiptoed closer, and in a well-practiced move, she turned her oldest around, smiling when he mumbled in his sleep. She lightly kissed each of them and then watched them sleep for several minutes.

Her love for them swelled inside her. These boys were her life. The best of her and Seth combined to create these wonderful little humans, and she would do anything to protect them. She saw little bits of Seth in the way Benjy smiled with one eyebrow lifted, and the way Jacob's hair swirled in two directions at the crown of his head. Even after two years, she still couldn't believe her husband and father of her children was really gone. And in such a shocking way. Without a moment's warning, she had joined a club of women who were working every day to hold a family together all on their own.

Even when I'm exhausted.

If things with Damon went beyond his day of babysitting, she'd make it clear she was not looking for a boyfriend. The last thing she needed was another male to take care of.

She slipped quietly from their bedroom and undressed before grabbing her pajamas. A hot shower relaxed her, and she couldn't wait to fall into her bed.

"Mama," Jacob called from across the hallway.

She sighed and turned off the bathroom light, heading for their room rather than her own.

Chapter Three

The out-of-tune melody of Damon's doorbell woke him way before he wanted to open his eyes. Just one more thing in his outdated house that needed replacing. When he convinced himself that the sound was part of a dream and rolled over, someone started knocking on his front door.

"This better be something good."

He climbed out of bed with a groan, pulled on a pair of athletic shorts and made his way through the dining room to the front door. Glancing through the peephole, he saw his brother Linc. He groaned even louder because he had a feeling he knew exactly what this early-morning visit was about.

With a frustrated twist, he unlocked and opened

the door. "Why are you here so early? You know I worked late."

Linc hitched a thumb toward the shiny new car in the driveway. "What's that?"

"It's a car that won't break down on the side of the road." Damon had known this was coming, but did it really have to be this early in the morning and before his coffee? He left the door open and turned for the kitchen, knowing his brother would follow.

"Did you get your inheritance check and not tell any of us?"

"Nope." He pushed Start on the coffee maker. "How did you find out about my new car?"

"I was driving by and saw it." Linc sat in one of the creaky chairs around the hand-me-down kitchen table.

Damon really wished he'd already fixed his garage door, so he could've parked his new car out of view.

"At first, I thought it might be a woman who stayed over, but your truck wasn't here. And the way you looked at Sari last night, I didn't think you'd brought someone else home."

His brother had that part right. Sari was the only woman on his mind. The only one he had a desire to bring home.

"This isn't how Mom raised us. What do you think she'll say?" Linc asked him.

"I'm sure she'll have plenty of opinions to give, as usual."

"You could always sell your house and move in with Mom," Linc said, unable to keep a straight face.

"Shut it, dude. Not funny." Their mom had done the best she could raising five children alone, but having a husband walk out the door when you were pregnant with your fifth child would make anyone rigid about routines and a little bitter. He barely remembered their father, Rick Maloney, who had also grown up without a dad around.

"You can't be spending money you don't have. What if for some reason your check never comes?"

A cold wave slapped him, and Damon glared at his oldest and bossiest brother. He hadn't even considered that possibility. "Why in the hell would you say that? Do you know something I don't?"

"No. I'm just making a point. You need to be patient, little brother. Buying big things on credit is not how we were raised."

The rush of panic eased, but a new whisper of "what if" hovered in his head. "You already said that. And it's easy for you to say that *now*. You aren't having to live like we used to. None of y'all are." He poured a cup of coffee and motioned for Linc to grab a mug. "Do you know what it's like watching all of you live it up and be able to buy things for Mom while I have to scrimp and save to make ends meet?"

Linc poured coffee into a Chatelaine Fire Department mug, added a spoonful of sugar and seemed to be truly considering this concept.

Damon took a healthy swallow of morning pick-me-up. "I broke down on the side of the road the other day, and it was going to cost a bundle to get repairs, and they would only have been a patch job."

"How are you going to make the car payments when you have house payments and the cost of renovations?" Linc waved his hand to encompass the flashback-in-time kitchen. The yellow countertops and harvest gold built-in double oven. The brightly colored fruit-print textured wallpaper that Damon had started peeling off around the pantry door.

"I'm putting off the renovations for now and I'll work extra shifts if I have to." And he'd rack up the balance on his credit card in hopes of being able to pay it off sooner rather than later.

"Just put a pause on buying anything else big." The piece of folded cardboard used to level the table legs had been dislodged and the table wobbled, sloshing coffee over the rim of Linc's mug. "You should've bought furniture instead of a car."

"Linc, I'm not your kid brother anymore. I can handle my own life."

"Habit, I guess." They were quiet for a few minutes while they drank their coffee.

Damon rubbed his bare foot over the textured vinyl flooring that he couldn't wait to replace. But he could live with it for a while longer if he had to. "Speaking of renovations, how's the bookstore coming along?"

"Great. We're almost ready to open. Remi's big ideas for the children's book section will be worth the extra time and effort. Kids are going to love it. So, are you really going to babysit for Sari?"

"Yes. I lost our bet. I have to." He didn't mention that he wanted to hang out with her kids because he wanted to get to know their mom.

Linc's phone chimed with a text message, and he pulled it out to look at the screen. "I need to get going. I'm late."

"Maybe you shouldn't have stopped to nag your brother like an old woman."

"Nah. Sounds boring." Linc put his mug in the sink. "See you later."

Damon continued to sit at his rickety table with the uneven legs. He'd been looking forward to putting his own touch on this house, but he had to have a car to get around. True, it didn't necessarily have to be a car as expensive as the one he'd bought, but it was too late now. He'd lose too much money if he traded it in so soon.

He looked around the room at all the things he'd planned to change. Like raising the dropped ceiling that was covered with foam rectangles more suited to an office than a home. He was tall and more height in the room would help it not to feel so closed in. And the popcorn ceilings in the rest of the house needed a good scraping. Especially the room with the blue shag carpeting that had glitter mixed in with the popcorn. He could save money by doing a lot of the demo himself. But then who knew how long he'd have to wait to buy materials, and until then, he'd have to live in a dismantled house.

He got up for a coffee refill and took out some of his frustration by ripping off another strip of wallpaper. It tore with a very satisfying sound.

When he opened his refrigerator for something to eat, there was a very limited and unappealing selection. He had a couple of pieces of toast with the last of the strawberry jam, then got dressed for a trip to GreatStore. Grocery shopping was something he hated and normally put off as long as possible, but today it came with the possibility of seeing Sari.

As Damon pushed his shopping cart up and down the aisles, he kept an eye out for the beautiful woman who had starred in his dreams last night. She'd said she was working today, but she had not been at a front register, so he kept searching. He tossed chips and other snacks in his basket along with frozen meals, cans of soup, bread and peanut butter, and other sandwich makings.

When he came around a freestanding display of bakery items, he spotted Sari in the produce section and a lightness filled his chest. She was arranging vegetables, and today she was wearing dark jeans. They weren't skintight, but they were definitely not "mom" jeans. She wore them well.

As he was pushing his shopping cart over to where Sari worked, a woman he'd gone out with a couple of times waved from across the display of bananas.

Oh, man. Not now.

She headed his way. "I'm so happy to see you, Damon."

When she said his name in a voice too loud for the store, Sari turned her head and looked right at him just as he received a very enthusiastic hug. One he ordinarily would have welcomed, but not today. Not in front of a woman he was hoping to get to know better.

Sari jerked her head back to her work. Maybe she was jealous and didn't like seeing him with another woman. He could hope.

"You, too," he said to the woman hanging on to him. "How have you been?"

"Good. I'm starting at a new hospital in Dallas next week."

She continued talking about her nursing job, but he was only half listening. Something about this re-union happening in front of Sari made him edgy and uncomfortable. Sari didn't seem like the kind of woman who had time for a man who dated a lot of different women.

But that's who I am. That's what I do.

He shook off that thought for later consideration. "I'm glad you're excited about your new job."

He was anxious for this surprise meeting to end so

he could talk to Sari before she disappeared to another part of the store. Thankfully, the interaction was brief and didn't involve any more hugging. When he made it over to Sari, he was relieved when she turned and gave him a big smile.

"Hi, Damon."

"Good morning."

She leaned forward to study the items in his cart. "I hope you're in this section of the store because you plan to add at least a few healthy items to your cart."

"What?" he said in mock outrage. "You don't approve of my meal choices?"

"Well…there is room for improvement."

"I'm not the best cook in the world. So I'm kind of limited on what I buy." He pointed to an eggplant. "Take that for example. I would have no idea what to do with that."

"I guess that vegetable can be a bit of a challenge." She continued arranging the squash. "I make a pretty good eggplant Parmesan."

"Sounds like something I need to try." He grabbed a bag of the small easy-to-peel oranges and added them to his cart.

"Is that a subtle hint? Are you asking me to cook for you?"

He chuckled. "No, but I wouldn't turn down an invitation."

"You never know. It could happen." She dropped a couple of zucchini squash into a plastic bag and put them into his cart. "Chop these into bite-sized pieces, then sauté them with a little olive oil and whatever seasoning you like."

"Sounds easy enough." Her concern about his health made him smile. No one had looked out for his eating since he'd lived under his mom's roof.

"Are you by any chance available to babysit this Saturday during the day?"

"I work Friday night, but I'm off on Saturday and would be happy to babysit. What do you have planned?"

"Alana asked me to do something with her, and I thought it might be a good chance for you to fulfill your promise. If you really are available."

"I am one hundred percent available," he said. "In every way."

Sari tried to hide her smile. "Cool. Is ten in the morning too early for you?"

"I can be there at ten. No problem." Before he could say more, a store manager was walking by and paused long enough to give Sari a look that Damon read as "get back to work."

"Text me your address because I better get out of here."

"I will."

As he pushed his cart toward the checkout, he overheard, "Sari, can I see you in my office?"

Damon winced, hoping he hadn't gotten her into trouble.

Chapter Four

"Benjy Keeling, do not even think about trapping your little brother under that laundry basket."

Her four-year-old froze with the plastic lattice-work basket hovering above his younger brother. Sari took it from him, and not for the first time, she considered canceling her day out with Alana. Leaving her boys with Damon was just asking for trouble of one kind or another.

"But Mama, he's a tiger," Benjy said with his hands held out like it should be totally obvious. "In zoos there's cages."

Her two-year-old, Jacob, shook his head of red curls and growled.

Sari chuckled and put the basket on the couch, loving that her boys were so good at playing pretend.

"I can see that. Very fierce. Instead of a cage, what if you use your blocks to build a wall around Jacob the tiger?"

Benjy bounced on his toes. "A magic wall so he can't climb it?"

"What a good idea." She kissed the top of his head and ruffled Jacob's hair, making him growl again.

A knock at the door sent her pulse tripping.

He's early.

It was too late to call Damon and say she'd changed her mind. Sari peered through a crack in the vertical blinds. With his thumbs snagged in the back pockets of his jeans, Damon's shoulders were drawn back, enhancing the way his black T-shirt pulled taut across a broad chest and stretched around his biceps. A dark lock of his hair fell over his forehead, the morning sun making it shine. It was entirely possible he was going to be the one who caused trouble, not her toddlers. And she had a feeling she'd be the one who caught that trouble.

Her emotions had been close to the surface all morning, but now she was practically vibrating. Sari smoothed a hand over her hair and opened her front door. "Good morning."

"Hi, Sari." Damon took a step closer. "It's good to see you again."

"You, too." His laid-back grin managed to be both easygoing and a bit mysterious. Some might even use the word *sexy.* No wonder women chased him down

in public to hug him. With no idea what he was thinking—and praying he couldn't read *her* thoughts—
she told herself to calm down and go on with today's
plans. Everyone said Damon was a good guy and
they would trust him to look after their own children.
She'd only be gone for a few hours.

"Have you changed your mind?" he asked.

"Oh, no. Sorry. Please come in." She stepped back
and ushered him inside while heat washed over her
face and neck. She'd been too busy overthinking and
staring at him and of course managed to embarrass
herself right out of the gate.

Her living room suddenly felt too small. Sensations she had attributed to a rare night out, a handsome man flirting with her and a couple of drinks
were once again flooding through her system. Without any of that, her attraction to him was just as
strong as it had been on Tuesday night. And after
her imagination had run wild over the last few days,
possibly stronger.

"Are you sure you're ready for this?" she asked him.
"You haven't changed *your* mind?"

"Nope. I'm ready to give a busy mom a much-
needed break."

That sweet statement touched her heart. Her boys
walked into the room and came over to stand on either side of her, staring at this man much like she
had done.

"This is Benjy, and this is Jacob." She put a hand on each of their heads in turn.

Damon knelt in front of them. "Hey, guys. I'm Damon. Can I hang out with y'all today?"

Jacob wrapped his arms around her leg and looked up at her in that way that told her he was nervous about her leaving. She picked up her baby for a cuddle and kissed his forehead.

Benjy cocked his head. "You know how to play superhero?"

"Of course." Damon stood.

"Okay." Benjy grabbed Damon's hand, ready to pull him down the hallway to their bedroom.

"Wait," she said to her son. "I need to talk to Mr. Damon for a few minutes. Why don't we all sit down and get to know one another." She sat on one end of her gray couch and Damon sat on the other.

Jacob got comfortable on her lap and rested his head against her chest but kept a close eye on the new guy while Benjy started digging in a basket of toys in the corner.

"I hope I didn't get you into trouble at work yesterday. I couldn't help overhearing her asking you to come to her office."

"No, you didn't get me into any trouble. I had asked about how I might work up to a management position, and she was giving me some information. I can't keep going from one menial low-paying job to another. Eventually, I want to go back to college and finish the last two years of my accounting degree."

"Sounds like a very good plan."

"You mentioned growing up in a big family," Sari said. "I'm an only child and have always been fascinated with what it's like to have siblings. There are four of you?"

"Five. You know Linc. He is the oldest. Next is Max, who I don't think you've met, and then Coop and me. We have one little sister, Justine. She was a single mom for most of her son's first year, and we were raised by a single mom. My dad was not around."

That's likely how he'd known she needed a break. She adjusted Jacob on her lap. "From what I can see so far, your mother did a good job."

"Thanks. Do you have family close by?"

"No. My parents were older when they had me. My mom was forty-five and my dad was fifty. I lost both of them within the last several years."

Benjy brought a book over and handed it to Damon. "Can you read?"

"I sure can."

With both hands on his hips, Benjy tipped his head. "Prove it."

Damon chuckled, but Sari gasped. "Benjy, you know that is not the way we talk to people. Especially not when you are asking for something."

"That's what the kids say at day care. They say, 'prove it' and 'don't be a chicken.'"

Sari hated that her kids had to go to day care, but she had no other option. The day care at GreatStore was the only one in her price range—unless she dipped into the money that she was saving for a rainy day. She knew better than a lot of people that you never could tell when a rainy day might turn into a flood. She had to stay prepared.

"Benjy, those are not things you say to an adult. Want to try again and ask Mr. Damon in a nice way?"

"Okay, Mama. Will you read to us, Mr. Damon?" Her sassy-pants four-year-old shot her a brief glance, then added one more thing to his request. "Please."

"I would be happy to read to you. Hop up here between me and your mom."

With more skill and flourish than she had expected, Damon read the short book about farm animals, making the boys giggle with his dramatic voices.

"The end," he said, and closed the book.

"Thank you." Benjy slid off the couch. "Gotta go potty."

Sari shifted her son on her lap. "Speaking of that. Jacob is doing really well with potty training, but he is still in Pull-Ups. You should ask him to try going potty about every thirty minutes."

"Good to know. And that's no problem. I've looked after my sister's son, Morgan."

"They live here in Chatelaine?"

"No. They live a few hours away in Rambling Rose, so I don't get to see them as much as I'd like."

With each minute they talked, and his willingness to share his life and family, she was feeling better about letting him babysit.

Jacob scooched off of her and crossed the center cushion to sit on Damon's lap. "Hi," he said in his cute baby voice.

"Hello, little buddy," Damon replied. "I like your green shirt."

Her youngest son did not take easily to many people, so this was a good sign, and she let herself relax a bit more.

Benjy came back into the room. "Now is it time to play?"

"Almost. Why don't you go get things ready in your room, and we will come find you before I leave."

Benjy took off down the hallway, but Jacob stayed on Damon's lap.

"You're worried about leaving, aren't you?" Damon said.

"Maybe a little."

"Please don't worry. We will get along fine. Like I said, I'm just a big kid myself."

She chuckled. "Is that supposed to make me feel better?"

"A very responsible kid." His teasing smile shifted into an understanding expression. "Sari, if you're truly not comfortable with this, we can cancel. The last thing I want to do is stress you out."

"A single mom is stressed out most of the time."

"I'm sure we can come up with some other way for me to pay my debt to you."

She could think of a few creative ways that would be fun for both of them. The direction her thoughts were taking with this man was an ill-advised path. "Since your references check out, I'm going to go ahead with my plans. I could use a break."

"Good call. You have to take care of yourself if you're going to be in any condition to take care of others."

"That is true. Let me show you where everything is." When she stood, Jacob raised his arms to her, as if still wary about her leaving. She lifted him from Damon's lap and walked into the open-concept kitchen with her toddler on her hip. A handwritten schedule was held on to the refrigerator door with musical note magnets. "Here is their schedule and all the important numbers like Poison Control. Call me if anything happens or you have questions." She paused and looked him straight in the eye. "Why are you grinning at me like that?"

"No specific reason. You just make me smile." He used a pointer finger to tickle Jacob's tummy and made him giggle.

Needing some physical distance from his enticing leather and spices scent, she opened the refrigerator door as a barrier between them and tapped a finger on a stack of three plastic containers. "This is lunch for all three of you."

"You made lunch for me, too?"

"I did. I hope you like peanut butter and jelly." She pointed to another shelf. "And here are some sliced apples."

"Got it. No ordering pizza and beer." He was close enough that Jacob reached out to him, and Damon took him into his arms. "Are you ready to have some fun today, little buddy?"

Her baby nodded and stuck his thumb in his mouth.

He looked so small against Damon's broad chest. Since her kids didn't have a man or any father figure in their lives, this was an unusual sight. One she ached for her boys to have.

"What are your plans for the day?" Damon asked, breaking into her thoughts.

"A haircut and pedicure with Alana."

He gasped in a dramatic fashion that made Jacob giggle again. "You aren't cutting off your hair, are you?"

"No, just a trim. Don't forget that you can call me at any time." She grasped his arm. "I'm serious. Call me straightaway if you have any questions at all or if there is any problem. Even a small one."

He put his free hand on top of hers, and that's when she realized her fingers were wrapped around his wrist. She relaxed her grip and pulled away.

"Don't worry. I promise I'll call you if we need you."

"Mama," Benjy yelled from his bedroom. "Are you coming?"

She let out a slow breath and they all went down the hallway to the boys' room. "Benjy, what did I say about yelling in the house?"

"No yelling."

"That's right. The neighbors don't need to hear everything you say." She bent forward and opened her arms. "Give me a hug." Benjy hugged her, and she could feel his excitement to play with a new friend. She turned to give Jacob a hug, but with him in Damon's arms, she hesitated. Jacob leaned toward her, and she couldn't deny him a kiss. When she met Damon's brown eyes, he looked as if he was hoping for a kiss, too. And she was surprisingly tempted. Instead, Sari took a few steps backward, sending the message that there would be no kissing between the adults in the room.

"You two be good for Mr. Damon."

"We will, Mama," Benjy said, but the sideways glance and grin he gave Damon were a bit suspicious.

Jacob looked a little less sure about her leaving, but when Damon stuck out his tongue, then pulled each ear to make it go that direction before touching his nose to make his tongue disappear into his mouth, her two-year-old giggled.

"Have fun," Damon said to her, and the three of them waved as she went out the door of the bedroom.

"Mama said to be good, but does that mean I can't be the bad guy if we play pretend?"

"I think it's okay if it's pretend," Damon said.

Sari took a deep breath and locked the front door of her apartment behind her. The three of them had already taken to one another. They would be okay. She got into her ten-year-old blue Volvo and drove toward Alana's house.

I need to get my mind on something other than Damon.

Jacob wiggled to get down, and Damon set him on his feet beside his big brother. "What shall we do first?"

The four-year-old put his hands on his little brother's head. "We're playing zoo. Jacob is a tiger, and we have to build a magic wall so he can't get out and eat all the people."

Jacob dropped to all fours, growled and tried to bite his brother's leg.

"No biting." Benjy shook a finger at him.

"Do I get to be an animal, too?" Damon asked.

"Yes." Benjy turned in a circle as he talked. "What do you wanna be?"

"I want to be a polar bear."

"Okay. Do polar bears give rides on their backs? I like animal rides. Mama took us to ride a little horse at the fair. It went round and round." Benjy galloped around Damon in demonstration. "Next time I want it to go faster and faster."

Damon liked this kid's spirit. "Since I will be a well-trained bear, yes, I will give rides to kids at our zoo."

They used a variety of blocks and other toys to make the animal cages in the living room, and the boys magically changed back into people so they could have a ride on the polar bear's back. Damon's knees were beginning to hurt from crawling around with the added weight on his back, but their happy laughter and encouragement kept him going.

"Who is hungry?" he asked the boys.

"I am," Benjy said. "Can we have cake?"

"I don't think your mom left any cake, but we can pretend our peanut butter and jelly sandwiches are cake."

The little boy shook his head. "I don't pretend *that* good."

Damon chuckled and held Jacob's hand as they went into the kitchen for lunch. He once again looked at the handwritten schedule. Everything for Benjy was written in blue and Jacob's schedule was written with green ink. Very organized and thorough. Guess as a single parent, Sari had to be.

After handwashing, he got out the three containers with their sandwiches and the apple slices, poured drinks, and got everyone seated. He was very glad she had prepared lunch and he didn't have to cook. They talked about all the animals you could ride, and he only had to get up twice while they ate. Once for napkins, and then again to grab a towel when Benjy spilled his milk.

Damon helped Jacob down from his booster seat, took the plastic containers to the sink and started washing them out. While he was cleaning up from a lunch that got a little messier than he'd hoped, the boys played with the animal magnets on the lower half of the refrigerator, and he didn't notice when they moved to the pantry.

"It's snowing," Benjy announced in a loud voice.

"No," Jacob fussed.

Damon turned to see the boys standing in the open doorway of the pantry. With a big mischievous smile, Benjy was sprinkling a handful of flour on his little brother's head.

"Lots of snow," the four-year-old said.

Damon groaned. "Oh, no. Benjy, don't do that. Now we have another mess to clean up."

Jacob shook his head and ran to Damon with his arms up. "You're okay, little buddy." He picked him up and held him over the sink while dusting flour from his hair.

"Superhero time," Benjy announced.

"Not until we clean up the mess you've made. Can you get the broom, please?"

The little boy sighed dramatically as if this was the worst idea ever, but he did as he was asked.

Because Damon had not thought to wash the boys'

hands after eating, the broom handle was now sticky, and he had to clean that, too. Once the kitchen, pantry and children were clean, the three of them went to the boys' bedroom.

"Is it nap time?" he asked the boys in a hopeful tone.

"No. Superhero time." Benjy opened a drawer and started tossing costumes over his shoulder. "Which one you want?" he asked Damon.

"I don't think any of these will fit me. But we can come up with something." Damon pulled the top Batman sheet off one of the twin beds and tied it around his neck like a cape. "Is this good?"

Benjy shook his head and sat beside the pile of costumes. "You need more. Jacob, you be Cat Boy."

Damon helped Jacob into a black cat Halloween costume and buckled a plastic utility belt around his waist. "There you go, little buddy. Super Cat Boy."

The two-year-old got on all fours and started crawling around while meowing.

Benjy had his legs in the air as he pulled on a Spider-Man costume. "Mama said we can't have a real cat. No pets in the 'partment."

"That's too bad. I like cats, too," Damon said. "We had one when I was a kid. It was orange and had a crooked tail."

"I want a black cat," Benjy said.

Jacob shook his head. "No, no, no. Purpur cat."

"He means purple, but that's not a real thing," Benjy clarified.

Damon tapped a finger against his chin. "Are you sure? Maybe purple cats are just very rare."

"I don't think so. I've never seen a purple cat."

"Purpur cat," Jacob repeated.

"I'm shooting webs and flying," Benjy yelled, and started jumping on the bed.

As he attempted a leap from one twin bed to the other, Damon caught him midair and put him on the floor. "I bet you are not supposed to be jumping on the bed. Am I right?" He really did not want them getting hurt on his watch. Then he'd be the one in trouble and Sari would never want to go out with him.

The little boy fell back onto the bed. "No yelling. No jumping on the bed. No fun."

Damon covered his mouth to hide his amusement. "I think we can still have tons of fun. Can I be Superman?"

The four-year-old sat up and shook his head. "You're Superboy."

"Okay. Now, I need to add to my superhero costume, and I have an idea. I need to go to the pantry and get the tinfoil."

While they played, Damon couldn't help wondering where their father was. Was he part of their lives or was he completely out of the picture? He didn't feel comfortable asking the kids.

At nap time, the boys insisted he continue to wear

his superhero costume while he sat on the floor between their twin beds and read to them. Four books later, they were both asleep. He eased to his feet, then stepped out of their room, closing the door as quietly as possible. Hopefully he had time to clean up a bit before Sari got home. He wanted to show her he hadn't been kidding about being able to do this.

Soft female laughter made him turn with a jerk. Sari was standing at the end of the short hallway, and she was grinning from ear to ear.

Chapter Five

Sari wished she had a camera to capture this moment. Damon was standing outside the boys' bedroom door dressed in full superhero regalia. With a Batman bedsheet for a cape, her black scarf tied across his forehead and tinfoil wristbands, he was someone she wanted to spend more time with, and she had a feeling her children would as well. The undercurrent of worry that had followed Sari on her girls' day out began to melt away.

"The boys are asleep?" she whispered.

His startled expression morphed into a proud smile. "Yes, ma'am."

She motioned for him to follow her into the living room. Apparently, Damon had not been bluffing about his babysitting skills. "Looks like the three of you had fun today. Which superhero are you?"

He snatched her scarf off his head as if just remembering he was wearing it. "I wanted to be Superman, but Benjy said I had to be Superboy."

With a quick laugh, she sat on the edge of her comfy red reading chair and started unbuckling her sandals. "I was thinking Captain Kid."

He looked down at himself and then shrugged. "Told you I was just a big kid."

"But you got both of them to nap, and that's saying something."

"I'm a very competent, responsible kid." He untied the sheet, rolled it into an untidy bundle and put it on the couch, then unwrapped the tinfoil wristbands. "Maybe I should save these for another time."

"Maybe so."

Would it be so bad to have him around? Next time he played with the boys, she wanted to be with them.

Damon dropped onto the charcoal-gray couch and spread his arms across the back like he was planning to stay awhile. "You look more relaxed than when you left. And your hair is gorgeous."

"Thank you. They only cut off two inches. And I am feeling more relaxed." She held out one foot and wiggled her freshly painted toenails, a flashy teal that she wouldn't normally pick. "A foot massage will do wonders for tension."

"Noted," he said with a mischievous grin. His fingers flexed against the couch cushions as if thinking about giving her a massage right now.

A lovely tingle started in the arches of her feet and shimmered up her body. The thought of his strong fingers massaging her feet, or any part of her, was… more tempting than it should be. She was tempted to tuck her feet beneath her, but at the same time, she wanted to put them in his lap and ask for a demonstration.

There was zero doubt that Damon was a huge flirt, but he also wasn't just another good-time guy. Sari was unexpectedly charmed by this cute-and-he-knew-it guy. At the Valentine's charity auction, he'd strutted and put on a playfully flirtatious show for the crowd, and she had been tempted to bid on him, but a single mom couldn't be that frivolous with her money, even if it was for charity. She'd been shocked to feel a twinge of jealousy for the woman who had won the bid, even if she had been old enough to be his great-grandmother.

From what she had witnessed so far, he was a good person, but she couldn't put off talking to him about what could and could not be between them.

Damon ran a hand through his hair in a motion that made Sari think that he was as nervous as she was.

"I know you won our wager, but I'd still like to take you out to dinner," he said.

"That's not necessary." Her heart gave an extra-strong thump against her rib cage. She hadn't been asked out by someone she actually had a desire to go out with since her husband. The little catch that always appeared when she thought of Seth grabbed her. But it was getting better.

Even though she and Seth had mutually agreed they wanted the other to move on if something ever happened to one of them, she hadn't had the time, energy or heart for dating. She hadn't even considered it. Two boys were enough to contend with right now, and she didn't need to make it three. Her hands were full.

Damon cocked his head to one side and his wavy dark brown hair that was a touch messed up from the scarf fell over his forehead, and his chest inflated on a long inhale. "I think dinner is very necessary." Sitting forward, he braced his forearms on his knees.

He had a way of shifting closer without crowding her. Like he was asking to be let into her personal space but would wait for an invitation. But she heard the request loud and clear.

Am I ready for something casual?

Spending a little time with a nice guy didn't seem like too much to handle. They could keep things casual and fun.

"I don't have a babysitter for tonight. I was lucky to get my neighbor to watch them so I could go out with everyone from work on Tuesday." She stood and smoothed the skirt of her emerald-green linen dress. "I'm thirsty. Want something?"

"I could use a drink." He followed her into the kitchen. "I'd like to take all three of you out to dinner."

She laughed, then tossed him a cold plastic bottle of juice. "Have you ever tried to eat out at a restaurant with two toddlers?"

"Hmm. Good point." As if on cue, a chunk of peanut-butter-coated apple dropped from the ceiling and landed with a *thunk* on the kitchen table.

He grimaced, but they both laughed. "Sorry about that."

"My point is proven." Even after reminding herself why she shouldn't get involved with a man right now, she was enjoying his company and didn't want him to leave. "Maybe we could get takeout? I've heard there is a great barbecue place in town."

"Harv's. I can go pick it up in a while." He glanced over his shoulder at the toys scattered around the living room. "First, I should help you get this place cleaned up."

"We can wait until the boys are awake to pick up the toys," she said. "They should help."

"That's a good rule. But I don't think they can reach the ceiling." Damon wet a paper towel and stood on a chair to clean the ceiling while she wiped the spot where the apple had landed. He sat at the kitchen table and twisted the top off his apple juice.

Sari took the seat across from him. "Will Harv's have any sides that are green vegetables?"

"You probably won't count fried okra as a healthy vegetable."

"No, but I love fried okra. I can add to the barbecue with something I have here. I try to make sure the boys have a fruit and vegetable with dinner."

"What should we do until the boys wake up and it's time to eat?" he asked.

Sari had to duck her head and let her hair screen her face so Damon wouldn't see any clue of her sudden wave of desire.

Get your head out of la-la land. And think of something to say.

"We could clean out my closet or my pantry," she said as a joke.

"Oh, yeah. About that." Damon scratched his head. "I should probably tell you that while I was cleaning up after lunch"—he glanced up at the ceiling where the peanut butter had been—"which I obviously don't get a gold star for, the boys got into the pantry and Benjy sprinkled flour on Jacob's head. So Jacob's hair might be a bit...dusty. And possibly the pantry is, too."

A flutter of joy settled over her, and he looked surprised when she smiled. "I'm kind of glad to hear that you truly did get the full two-toddler experience."

"I believe I did, but we had fun, and nothing got broken. They're great boys. It's obvious you are a wonderful mom. Other than not letting them have a purple cat."

She laughed. "They told you about that?"

"Yes. In detail. That's when we were playing zoo."

"Someday I'll get them a cat. I'd actually like to have one myself."

"They really don't allow pets at this apartment complex?"

"Well, technically they do, but my neighbor Jim is the only one who has a dog. The pet deposit is outrageously expensive, which translates into the owners not really wanting pets on their property. My luck, the cat would pee on the carpet in every room, and I'd lose the deposit."

Damon tapped his index finger on the table. "I have a big yard now, and I've been considering getting a pet."

"Did you buy a house?"

"I did. It was built in 1972 and it's all original. And I do mean all. Well, except for most of the shag carpeting that has been removed."

"*Most* of it? You mean there's still some shag carpeting in your house?"

"Yep. There's still one guest room that is rarely used. The carpet is three shades of blue."

"Oh, wow. I've always been fascinated with that time period. I'd love to see your house."

A slow smile appeared. "Did you just invite yourself over to my house?"

She covered her mouth but then chuckled. "Sorry, no. I didn't mean to do that."

"No backing out now. Tomorrow you and the boys should come over and see the house. You can have the grand tour. We can order pizza, or I can make hot dogs."

Of course he would suggest pizza and hot dogs instead of healthy food. But…she did love pizza and rarely had it anymore. "I haven't had pizza in months."

"What?" His eyebrows arched comically. "You're kidding."

The perplexed expression on his face did make him look a bit like a kid. "No, I'm not kidding. But I think the boys would really like hotdogs…if I can bring a salad."

"It's a deal." He spread one tanned and long-fingered hand over his stomach. "All this talk of food is making me hungry."

"We can eat early." She walked over to the pantry, grabbed a granola bar and tossed it to him. "Will that satisfy you for now?"

"I suppose it will have to do…for now." One corner of his mouth slowly turned up.

His grin made her think he was talking about something other than food. What would it be like to kiss his full, flirty mouth? To keep from staring at him, she turned back to the open pantry and swiped her finger across a plastic container of cereal. There was a fine layer of flour, but he'd done a pretty good job cleaning up. She grabbed a small bag of nuts and dried fruit for herself and then sat across from Damon at her small kitchen table.

He tore open the wrapper of his granola bar. "You know, when you eat together, I think they call it a date."

"So you are counting this snack as a first date?" It was impossible not to return his smile.

"Second. I'm counting the pretzels and drinks we had on Tuesday night as our first date."

It actually had felt like a date even though it had been short. "Counting dates must be one of your other rules?" She popped an almond into her mouth.

"No, but now I'm adding it."

This handsome man was such a flirt, but he was so fun to talk to, and as it turned out, he was also good with kids.

Remember he is young and carefree and no doubt not looking to settle down with an older single mom of two kids.

She rubbed her cheeks with her palms. Why was her brain even bothering to consider any of this? She was definitely not ready for a romantic relationship. But he was so damn handsome.

"I can see you thinking over there," he said.

"Oh, yeah? What am I thinking?" *Please don't be a mind reader.*

"That when we have barbecue tonight, it will be

our third date. And you know what they say about third dates."

She laughed. "What do they say?"

"That it often comes with something at the end of the night."

That was not what she had been thinking, but now that he'd brought it up… She had the urge to fan her face, her mind going straight to scenarios it should not. But she'd opened the door and walked right into that answer.

With his elbows propped on the table, Damon leaned toward her. "A kiss." His voice was smooth and seductive.

A wave of tingles swept over her, and she chuckled awkwardly. Again, that was not what she had been thinking. This time she'd pictured them in bed. None of this was going according to plan. Her relationship with Damon was not supposed to be about counting dates to get to…intimacy.

"And the kiss can be anywhere you want it to be."

Her mouth dropped slightly open as another sweep of heat scorched her skin. Exactly where on her body was he suggesting? She really wanted to kiss him, and she was going to have a tough time getting the idea out of her head.

"The back of your hand, your cheek or of course, your lips if you prefer."

Oh, for the love— She wanted to cover her face and

shrink down in her chair. *I need to get my thoughts moving back in the right direction.*

She seemed to be jumping several steps ahead of Damon at every turn. "Hmm. Lots of choices. I'll have to give those options some thought between now and our third date this evening."

"Good answer. Feel free to let me know if you want to practice before then."

She laughed, but it sounded more like a giggle, and her lips tingled even though he wasn't even touching her. "Thanks for the offer."

He did not need to know how incredibly attractive she found him. And he definitely didn't need to know that she hadn't kissed anyone since becoming a widow a little over two years ago. Her next first kiss was a big deal to her because it meant starting a new chapter, and she wasn't ready to begin again.

But one kiss might be okay.

There was also the fact that she'd basically invited herself over to his house for another meal. What level was that on Damon's intimacy scale?

Chapter Six

Damon would never admit it, but babysitting toddlers was hard work, and he could use a nap himself. But the day had been fun, and he wasn't ready for his time with Sari to end. "I really will help you clean the pantry."

"Really? Prove it," she said, using the term Benjy had learned at day care.

Damon laughed but quickly covered his mouth so he wouldn't wake the boys. "Be careful what you dare me to do."

They ended up cleaning the pantry and talking about a wide range of topics from music to childhood experiences.

When they were finishing, Damon put the boxes

of pasta back on the shelf. "Have you done much traveling?"

"No. I haven't left the US. Have you?"

"No, but I plan to. I want to visit lots of countries and experience different cultures. Swim in a few different oceans and try out things I don't even know about yet."

"I hear one of the boys waking up," she said.

Damon cocked his head to try to catch a sound but couldn't. "Must be your mom senses."

"Mama." Jacob was rubbing his eyes as he walked into the kitchen. He looked at each of them as if he'd forgotten Damon was here and then went to his mother.

"Hey there, sweet boy." She lifted him onto her lap for a hug. "Did you have a good nap?"

The toddler yawned and rubbed his face against her shoulder. He turned in her arms and smiled shyly at Damon.

A child's genuine smile was the best. "Should we tell your mama what a good boy you were all day?"

He tipped his face up to Sari and whispered, "Good boy."

"I'm so proud of you. I knew you'd have fun."

"No Benjy," Jacob said, and rubbed his little hand over his red hair.

"Oh, my. Your brother wasn't a good boy?"

The toddler shook his head. "No good, Mama."

Damon covered his chuckle with a throat clearing. Had he tattled on his older brothers at this age? "Benjy did just fine. From my personal experience, it's just what brothers do."

A few minutes later, Benjy joined them in the kitchen. "You're still here," he said to Damon.

"I am. I thought I'd stay for dinner. I'm going to go get barbecue, so your mama doesn't have to cook." That was true, but selfishly, he was enjoying his time with Sari and her boys and wanted to stay longer and get to know them better.

A little while later, Damon put two take-out bags on Sari's kitchen counter beside the sink. *Harv's New BBQ* was written across the side. Sari had cut fruit into child-sized bites and put it onto four plates. Apparently, he was eating apples, bananas and grapes whether he liked it or not. And he kind of liked it. It felt like he was one of her boys.

"They were running a special and gave us free brownies," he said.

Benjy gasped, and his eyes lit up. "Brownies?"

"Yep. One for each of us," Damon said.

Sari sighed and worried her lower lip with her teeth. "You can have a small one if you eat all of your fruit first."

"Yay! I'm gonna tell Jacob." The little boy ran from the kitchen.

Damon had a feeling that he was now the one who

wasn't being a good boy. "Should I not have said anything about the brownies?"

"It's okay. You didn't know that I limit their sugar intake."

"I did notice there weren't any sweets in the pantry while we were cleaning up the flour."

"Eating a healthy diet is very important."

He caught a flash of emotion that he read as pain before she quickly ducked her head. There had to be a good reason for her reaction, but it was way too soon to pry any deeper. "Easter is coming up, and there will be candy everywhere. What happens then? Do you celebrate Easter?"

"We do, and I do let them have candy on holidays. I'm not a total monster." She winked at him.

"I would never think such a thing." But he did think she was a bit strict with their diets. Sari was not going to approve of the candy he had in his pocket. Thankfully he had not given them any since hard candies were choking hazards for children as young as her boys.

Once plates were filled and kids were in their booster seats, they sat together at the four-person table that was nicer than the old one in his kitchen. This was like no third date Damon had ever been on. He'd dated a few women with kids, but they had never hung out together like… Something swelled in his chest, then tightened around his lungs. *Like a family. Growing up without a father, he'd always thought two parent households were something only other people had.*

"This is really good barbecue. I'm glad you suggested it." She put another bite into her mouth, then licked sauce from her lower lip.

He was momentarily mesmerized by the sweep of her tongue combined with such a satisfied expression. "Yes, very good."

Benjy put a piece of fried okra on the spoon resting on the edge of his plate, and then he hit the spoon, launching it across the table to hit the refrigerator. He covered his mouth but giggled behind his hand.

Damon bit the inside of his cheek to keep from laughing. It was totally the kind of thing he would have done at Benjy's age. Even now, he felt an inappropriate urge to do the same thing, just to see if he could make his land in the sink.

"Benjy, do you want a brownie?" Sari asked calmly.

The little boy sat up straighter. "Sorry, Mama. I want a brownie."

Damon and Sari shared a smile.

"Me brownie," Jacob echoed his brother's desire.

The rest of the meal was filled with laughs and a conversation about cats. Once he couldn't eat another bite and the little boys' faces were covered with chocolate, Damon put his plate in the sink. "You go do bath time or whatever you need to do for the boys, and I'll clean up and put the leftovers away," he said.

"Thanks. I'll take you up on that." She paused and looked back at him. "And I'll see you after I get them tended to?"

"I'll be here."

Sari held out her hands to her children. "Come on, you two. It's bath time for stinky little boys."

"Not tinky," Jacob said.

"Well, you are sticky, so let's get cleaned up and put on your pajamas so you can watch an episode of *PAW Patrol* before bedtime."

That got their attention, and Sari followed them from the room, but she shot him a smile over her shoulder.

While cleaning up, Damon took his time putting plates in the dishwasher and leftovers in the refrigerator. He didn't mind waiting for them to tend to their nighttime routine. There was nothing for him to rush home to except a three-bedroom house with no one in it but him. Not even a fish in a bowl. Maybe he should get a pet. He could use a little more excitement in his house.

Once he had his house remodeled, he was going to throw some killer parties, and his home would be filled with life. He'd already had offers from five women to help him "decorate" the master bedroom. But he'd only had one woman over to his house so far, and Katie had moved away for a job.

The boys ran back into the kitchen, and without watching where he was going, Jacob smacked his forehead on the kitchen tabletop. He plopped onto his little bottom and immediately started to cry.

Before Damon or Sari could get to him, Benjy rushed forward. "It's okay, Jacob. I'll make it better." He held his little brother's cheeks and kissed his forehead like he'd no doubt seen his mama do. "All better?"

"Yes," Jacob said, but his lower lip wobbled as if he wasn't so sure.

Sari knelt in front of Jacob. "Let Mama make it better, too." She kissed his forehead and then drew both boys into a hug. "I love you both so much."

It was the most touching scene Damon had seen in a long time. Benjy might occasionally torment his younger brother, but he balanced it out with his sweet and caring nature. Damon remembered being protective and looking out for his little sister when they were small.

Once she got her kids settled down and watching their cartoon, Sari motioned to the couch. "Do you have time to sit and talk for a few more minutes?"

"You bet." There was a noticeable shift in her demeanor. A nervous sort of seriousness that put him on high alert and made his chest tighten.

Please don't let this be her saying that we can only date if I don't date anyone else.

He'd heard that request a time or two and had quickly and politely declined to continue dating those women. He really hoped it was not going to happen in this case.

Damon loved women and knew how to be kind and considerate. He also knew how to let them know up front that he wasn't looking for anything serious. That's probably why he'd remained on good terms with most of his exes. Although he wanted a family someday, he was not looking to settle down anytime soon.

Then why have I put off a conversation I usually have right away? Why am I talking about third dates and kisses before we've had the casual relationship conversation?

If this wasn't the topic she was about to bring up, he'd find a way to do it himself. They had to be on the same page—or at least in the same book—moving forward.

"I need to…" She glanced at her kids and then lowered her voice. "I need to tell you that I am not looking for a relationship right now."

Relief eased the tension that had gathered between his shoulder blades. "That's cool. We're in agreement. I'm not looking for anything serious, either." He had too many plans to enjoy the hell out of single life once he became a millionaire. "I know how to do casual. In fact, I've been called Mr. Casual a time or two."

Sari's eyebrows rose slightly. "The only commitment I can make right now is to my children. They are where my focus and energy must go."

"Completely understandable. Another clue that you are a wonderful mother." For him the matter was settled, but the way she was picking at her fingernail, he sensed that she wanted or maybe even needed to say more.

"I'm not in a position to juggle a romantic relationship on top of everything else going on in my life." She sat straighter and rushed to say more. "But I've got it all handled. I don't want this to come off as me struggling to take care of my kids or myself. I've always been a very independent woman and that is not going to change."

"Noted and admired." He rested his arm on the back of the couch but stopped just shy of touching her. "In the short time I've known you, I can tell you're a strong woman who has it all together. For example, your multicolored schedule for the boys is genius."

"Thanks. It's nice to hear when someone recognizes my strengths. I hate it when people think I need looking after like I'm a child." Sari rubbed her palms against her thighs. "I'm just not comfortable getting into a relationship right now. My last one ended…" She cleared her throat. "It was, well, horrible."

Damon's relief turned to concern, and he had the urge to draw her into his arms and comfort her, but her body language kept him on his end of the couch.

It must have been a bad divorce, and he wondered once again where the man was. "I'm really sorry to hear that."

She waved a hand in tandem with her shaking head. "But I don't like to talk about that."

Another thing to note. Tread carefully around the subject of her ex. He wouldn't bring it up unless she did. "Since we're on the same page about relationships, what do you think about agreeing to just hanging out?"

Her sigh was one of relief. "Hanging out. No commitments?"

"No commitments. Just casual fun."

"I can do that. I like fun."

And he liked the sound of that. A lot. Before he thought to stop himself, he reached for her hand on the cushion between them and gave her fingers a light squeeze and was rewarded with her smile that had slipped away a moment ago.

"So, is your last name Fortune or Maloney?"

"I guess you've heard about the unusual Fortune inheritance?"

"Only a little. It's hard not to in this small town. If you don't mind sharing, what's the deal with that?"

"I've been a Maloney my whole life. My father, Rick Maloney, was also raised by a single mom and never knew who his father was. His mother gave him her maiden name, but recently we've learned that my dad's real father was the late Wendell Fortune. He was one of the owners of the silver mines in the area. His best friend, Martin Smith, found my little sister, Justine, in Rambling Rose, and when he thought she was getting married because she needed someone to support her and her son, he gave her a large inheritance check."

She tucked her feet beneath her and faced him. "Wow. Did she get married?"

"Yes. To her son's father. They seem very happy and in love."

"A surprise inheritance. That's the kind of thing everyone dreams about, and it happened to you all for real."

"Well, it hasn't happened to me yet."

"Oh, I figured that's how you were able to buy your house."

"I had to get a loan. I bought it from the man who had it built. He and his wife were a great couple. I took care of their yard for years and did odd jobs around the house. She passed away a couple of years ago, and he recently moved into assisted living."

They continued talking about the unusual way each of his siblings had become wealthy one by one.

The boys' cartoon ended, and Benjy jumped up. "Mr. Damon, can you play Hungry Hungry Hippos one time before we have to go to bed?"

He looked at Sari and at her smile and nod, he answered the little boy. "Sure. I haven't played that game in a long time."

* * *

Sari curled up on the couch and watched Damon on the living room floor with her kids. All three of them were on their tummies while they played the noisy game where they pushed a lever as fast as they could to make their hippo gobble up the most marbles. And as expected, they ended up playing more than one game.

When Jacob rolled onto his back and yawned, she looked at her watch. "It's past your bedtime, and if you want a book before bed, we need to go now."

"Mama, not yet," Benjy said.

"No, no bed," Jacob said, and yawned again.

"Do I have to go to bed, too?" Damon asked.

His mischievous smile sent tingles rushing across her skin. "Yes, I believe you do, too."

"What if I read you one story before I go home?" Damon said.

"Okay." Benjy stood and held out a hand to his little brother. "Let's pick books."

"One book," Sari called after them.

They followed the boys into their bedroom, and Damon sat on the floor between their beds while Sari sat on the foot of Jacob's bed. The boys once again loved his funny character voices. She did, too.

He read the last page and closed the book. "All right, you two. Time to say good-night." He ruffled each boy's hair.

"Sweet dreams. Mama loves you both so much."

She gave them good-night kisses and tucked the covers around them then switched on the nightlight, and they left the room.

As they walked back to the living room, she let her shoulder brush against his arm, but her nerves were kicking up, making her stomach do flips. When they stopped beside the door, she took hold of his hand and gave it a squeeze. "Thanks again for babysitting and for dinner."

He brought her hand to his lips and kissed the back of it, but he didn't let go. When he tipped his head to smile at her, his wavy dark hair fell over his forehead.

At this moment, she couldn't think of one single reason why kissing him was a bad idea. Especially when it was something they both wanted.

"Good night." Damon released her hand and turned for the door.

"Wait." She took a step closer. Close enough to let him know it was okay, and what's more, that she wanted to kiss him. "Don't go yet."

Chapter Seven

Staring into Sari's big blue eyes, Damon felt his pulse pound faster and faster as he waited for her to say more. Why didn't she want him to go? Kissing Sari was forefront in Damon's mind. He longed to discover whether her lips were as soft as they looked and what kind of kiss it would take to make her sigh. What kind of wonderful female sounds would she make if he kissed her deeply?

Sari shifted nervously and briefly glanced toward her boys' bedroom. "Thank you for being so good to my children."

"You're welcome. They're great kids." Normally by this stage, he would kiss her goodbye without hesitation, but Sari deserved his patience. Even though she seemed willing, if it was nothing more than his own lust making him misread her signs, it could mess things up. For tonight, he wouldn't risk it.

Waiting would give him something to look forward to. Delayed gratification was supposed to be good, right? He'd keep telling himself that.

He grasped the doorknob, ready to turn it. "Are we still on for you three coming over to my house tomorrow?"

She hesitated as if deciding what to say, and then closed some of the distance between them.

He held his breath and swayed forward, and not wanting to misread the moment, he waited a heartbeat, but her lips didn't meet his. Instead, her cheek brushed feather soft against his, her lips so achingly close as she kissed his cheek then stepped back before he had time to take things further.

"Yes. We'll be there. Good night, Damon."

"Sweet dreams." He reached out and brushed his knuckles over her soft cheek and then opened the door. He'd never been so turned on by a barely-there kiss.

A few steps away from her door, he nodded to a guy who must be the dog owner Sari had mentioned. His small terrier pulled at his leash and yipped. He'd seen the man—whose name he thought was Jim— around town but didn't know him. And he definitely didn't like the way Jim was currently glaring back and forth between him and Sari's door.

"Did you just come from Sari's apartment?" the man asked.

He was tempted to be snarky and say that he had watched him come out of her door and knew the answer to his own question, but he decided to see where this was going. Was he in competition with her next-door neighbor? The way the other man's eyes narrowed it was likely the case. "Yes, I did."

"Sari is a single mom, and she's new in town. I look out for her."

He recalled Sari's words about hating it when people thought she needed looking after. "Cool. Have a good night." Damon spun on his boot heel and headed for his car without looking back at the man. He could have warned the guy that painting her as a helpless woman was not going to go over very well, but he decided to let him discover that all on his own. But that didn't keep him from wondering about the nature of their relationship.

A growl rose in his throat. Why was he feeling so jealous when only minutes ago he'd been relieved Sari wanted to keep things casual? As he pulled out onto the road from her parking lot, he caught a glimpse in his side mirror of Jim knocking on her door.

"Again, Mama. Play it again."

Sari hit Repeat on her car stereo and song number five on the Kidz Bop CD started over—for the third time. But she couldn't help smiling at her boys in the rearview mirror. Their singing was one of the cutest things ever. With directions that consisted of only three turns, getting to Damon's house was simple, but figuring out what she was going to do with the guy was a different story. She was tempted to find a longer route just to give herself more time to settle her nerves.

While the boys continued serenading her, she replayed some of last night's conversation with Damon, for about the tenth time. When she'd told him she was not in the right place for a relationship, the goal had been for him to agree that was best. So why was she disappointed that he had agreed immediately and not fought her on it?

Because I'm so attracted to him.

She wouldn't have minded if he had been at least a little bummed about her not wanting to pursue a relationship.

As Sari pulled into the driveway in front of Damon's house, her eyes widened at the sight of the fancy silver sports car in the driveway. Not a very child-friendly car, but also not totally unexpected for Damon the charmer. The light tan brick house had a roofline with lots of angles, fitting the 1970s architecture. The front yard was well landscaped and tended with shrubs and flowering bushes. She couldn't wait to see inside.

Damon stepped out of his front door and waved.

In well-worn faded jeans and a black T-shirt, he once again gave off a bad-boy vibe. Or maybe it was more accurate to say a wannabe bad-boy vibe. She'd been around him enough to suspect he was more Prince Charming than rogue. At least she *thought* so.

"Mama, look. Mr. Damon," Benjy said, and started unbuckling the seat belt across his booster seat.

"I know, sweetie. This is his house."

Why am I here? I shouldn't be here.

But she was, and it was time to open her door and get out. With one more calming breath, she did just that.

"You look pretty today," Damon said as he flashed his Prince Charming smile.

"Thanks." She glanced down at her yellow sundress as Damon drew close enough that she could have hugged him, but when her pulse jumped in her throat, she turned to get the boys out of the car. "Your house is great."

Jacob knocked on his window, anxious for her to get him out of his car seat. She opened his door, put a backpack of toys over one shoulder, and then clicked the latch and lifted Jacob from his seat, but when she tried to put him down, he clung to her like a koala bear. Benjy scrambled out after them.

"Hey, boys. What's going on?" Damon asked.

"I was singin'," Benjy said, and did a funny little dance with spins and a few kicks.

"And what about you?" he asked Jacob. "Did you sing, too?"

He nodded and returned Damon's smile.

She kissed the top of her son's head. "All right, my little koala, I need to put you down so I can get the food from the front floorboard."

Jacob clung tighter, his shyness keeping him attached to her.

"I'll get it." Damon grabbed the ice chest on her floorboard and motioned for them to follow.

"I brought fruit salad and carrot sticks with homemade ranch made with Greek yogurt for dipping." Being a single parent was the reason she made sure to eat well and exercise. She had to stay healthy and strong for her kids, because if something happened to her... There was no good option for who would raise them. Her parents were gone, and Seth's father was older and not in great health. A few cousins in other parts of the country would not be ideal choices either.

"Come on in, and feel free to look around."

His front door opened into a small entry with a coat closet to the left, and across from it was a narrow bench in front of a feature wall made of wooden slats that you could see through into the raised living room. Under the bench were running shoes, hiking boots and a pair of flip-flops. She walked forward into an empty dining room, but it did have one wall of mirrors like a dance studio. Across from the mirrored wall was a bar, and a sliding glass door that led out to a covered patio and large backyard. There was no doubt about the era of the house. It screamed '70s.

He set her small cooler of food on the bar top.

She turned in a slow circle. "This house is set up in a way that begs for a party. Have you had many?"

"No, I haven't lived here very long, but I've been thinking about having a housewarming party."

"You definitely should."

Jacob wiggled in her arms. "Down, Mama."

She put him on his feet, and he joined his big brother dancing in front of the wall of mirrors.

If Damon didn't yet have his large inheritance like his siblings, how could he afford to pay for a house and his fancy car on a bartender's salary? Was he one of those people who bought way beyond their means? She had to be all about careful spending. "Do you just not have any dining room furniture, or are you using this as a dance studio?"

He chuckled and glanced at the boys singing and dancing without a care in the world. "No furniture, yet."

"This would be a great place to practice yoga."

"I've never done yoga." He braced a hand on the wall beside the sliding glass door. "You should come over and teach me sometime."

"Maybe I will." The thought of some of the partner positions they could get into made the warmth of a blush creep up her neck. She ducked her head, letting her long hair swing forward to hide her reaction.

"Want to see the rest of the house?"

"Please." She got her boys' attention. "Do you want to stay in here while I look around or come with us?"

"Stay," they both said, then sat on the floor of his empty dining room with their backpack of books and toys.

She followed Damon through the opening at one end of the mirrored wall to see two bedrooms with a bath between them. One room had only a double bed and nightstand, and the other was completely empty, except for the blue shag carpeting. "This is the original carpet you were talking about."

"Yep. I haven't decided whether to leave it or replace it."

"But you didn't tell me the walls were blue as well."

"I think I'll start calling it the blue room," he said.

Sari chuckled. "Very accurate name. Since it's in such good condition, I'd leave it for now. You could turn this room into a retro hangout space. I can picture beanbags, a record player, plants hanging in macramé holders and maybe even lava lamps."

"That's a good idea. If I take your suggestion, will you hang out in here with me?"

The mental picture of them sharing a beanbag sent lovely sensations zipping to several parts of her body. "We did agree to hang out."

"And to have fun," he said, his voice pitched low. "Can't forget you suggested the fun part."

His bedroom-eyes expression gave her a pretty clear idea of the kind of fun he was envisioning.

Or is it just my suddenly overactive imagination creating a fantasy?

The blue room seemed to be having a sudden heat wave, and she was tempted to fan herself, but instead she backed toward the door. "Show me the rest of the house."

She heard his soft chuckle as he followed her from the room. They crossed back through to check on the boys, who were stacking little wooden blocks and taking turns headbutting them so that they crashed onto the tile floor. "We're dinosaurs," Benjy said.

"Don't get too wild," she said. "I don't want to hear any dinosaurs crying."

"Dinosaurs don't cry, Mama."

"Oh, you're right. How silly of me."

Damon led her into what was obviously his bedroom. You couldn't actually call the room decorated. It was more like a bachelor pad with mismatched furnishings, but it was neat and clean. A king-size bed was centered on the back wall, and he was standing right in front of it. She had an inappropriate urge to rush forward, push him onto the mattress and straddle his muscular body. Being in this room with him wasn't helping her cool off. Not one little bit.

She turned away from him before she gave in to her desires and went into the en suite bathroom. The large shower and sunken tub combo was made of Carrara marble. The bathroom was spacious and luxurious but needed a female touch. "This is really nice. The boys would love that bathtub."

"Now, prepare yourself for the kitchen," he said. "Unfortunately, it's not open concept like so many newer homes. But maybe I can do something about that someday."

The boys had abandoned their blocks and were making funny faces in the mirror. Damon made a face at them that caused fits of little-boy giggles, and then he pushed through a swinging door into the kitchen off the dining room. It was the time warp he'd promised with loads of original style and features.

"Wow." She turned in a slow circle to take everything in.

He chuckled. "Is that a good wow or a 'what the hell'?—which is the way I feel about it."

"I love your house, but this room might be going a bit too far with the retro." The wood stain on the cabinets had aged to an orangish tint and the laminate countertops were bright yellow.

The boys joined them in the kitchen. "Mama, we're hungry. For brownies," Benjy said, and smiled at Damon hopefully.

Sari shot Damon a playful look that said "look what you've done," and he shrugged with a boyish grin of his own.

"Let's eat," he said.

They gathered the food and moved out into his backyard. Damon grilled hot dogs on his patio while the boys ran around in his large yard, empty except for a little white storage shed along the back fence, flower beds and a huge elm tree in the center.

They sat at a wooden picnic table that had seen better days and ate hot dogs, chips, fruit salad, and carrot sticks with homemade ranch dip.

After they ate, Sari cleaned up Damon's kitchen. Although it was way out of style, she marveled at what good condition the fiftysomething-year-old countertops were in.

She turned to find Damon leaning in the doorway to the dining room with a big grin on his face. "The boys are watching a cartoon in the living room."

"Good." She glanced at the clock on the wall above the table. "They'll probably fall asleep. At least Jacob will."

He crossed the room to stand near her. "What were you thinking about so hard?"

"Just marveling at this time capsule. They took excellent care of the place."

"Did I tell you that the couple who built this house were the only ones who ever lived here?"

"Yes, you did."

"From the age of fifteen, I used to mow their grass and help out around the house."

A sharp pain tugged at her heart. Every time someone mentioned mowing the grass, she thought of Seth and that tragic day.

"Would you consider helping me narrow down my choices for remodeling materials?"

She shook off the memory and focused on the present. "Sure. I've always wanted to design a house. What are you thinking about doing?"

"Something from this decade." He rubbed a hand over the spot where he'd started peeling off the wallpaper. "What would you do in here?"

"Pulling off the wallpaper is a good start. It's so dark in here and needs to be lightened up. Are the cabinets in good shape?"

"Yes." He opened one and knocked on a sturdy wooden shelf. "Solid wood and well built, but the style of the doors seems outdated."

"If it was my house, I'd paint the cabinets white or some other light color like pale blue."

"Or just get new doors," he said. "Once I have the money."

She had no idea how much inheritance each of his siblings had received but judging from the way the others had started living, it was a lot of money. "You definitely need to replace the laminate countertops with something like granite. Cover up or replace the avocado-green vinyl flooring with…almost anything."

He chuckled and stared down at the floor. "I one

hundred percent agree with that. There's room for an island in the middle, and I'm thinking of adding one."

"Excellent idea. You're lucky the former owners took such good care of the place."

"No doubt. They didn't have any children or anyone else to leave it to, and I think that's why he sold it to me way below market value. I couldn't have afforded it otherwise."

Probably because he bought that fancy sports car.

Sari was all about saving and careful spending. Living beyond your means was a certain recipe for disaster. She of all people knew how life could change in seconds. And that's why the life insurance money she received after Seth's death was in a savings account. It was there for emergencies, not frivolous spending. Thankfully, her car had been bought and paid for before she'd become a widow.

Jacob squealed, then started whining.

"Benjy," Sari called to them. "What's going on in there?"

"Nothing," he yelled back, and then both boys giggled.

"Taking down at least part of that wall to see into the rest of the house might not be a bad idea," he said.

"That's the truth. We better go check on them."

They crossed through the dining room and went up two steps into the raised living room. One side of the vaulted ceiling was angled. The far wall had a large brick fireplace surrounded by wide cedar boards attached to the wall at an angle to match the ceiling.

The boys were side by side on the sectional sofa with their attention glued to the cartoon on the flat-screen TV. Both of their eyes were starting to droop and flutter.

Damon sat on the couch, and she had no other seating option but to sit beside him.

"This carpet isn't as old as the shag, but it needs to go soon. Do you think it should be replaced with more carpet, tile or wood?"

"I'd definitely go with wood and area rugs. Then, you can easily change the style of the room with a new rug."

A few minutes later, the boys were both asleep.

"Can I ask you something?" Damon said, and stretched his arms above his head.

She caught a peek of his toned abs as his shirt rose above his waistband. "Sure."

"Why did you get a divorce?"

The question took her by surprise, and she was momentarily speechless. They had never specifically talked about it, but since Alana knew Seth had died, she assumed the information had made its way to Damon.

"I'm not divorced."

His mouth dropped open, then he snapped it shut. "You're still married?" he said under his breath, his eyes cutting toward the boys.

She clutched his hand when he started to stand up. "Damon, I'm a widow."

"Oh, honey. I'm so sorry." He clasped her hand between both of his. "I didn't know. Why didn't you tell me?"

"Alana knows, so I figured you knew, too. I wasn't trying to keep it a secret."

"When? How?" He shook his head. "I'm sorry. I shouldn't be asking you so many questions."

"It's okay. Right before Jacob was born." She pressed her fingertips to her mouth, and Damon seemed to realize that she needed just a moment.

"Forget I asked. I didn't mean to upset you or ruin the vibe of the day. Ignore me and my big mouth."

She looked up at him and forced a smile. "It's probably something we should talk about…at some point soon. That way you'll know where I am coming from and why I make the decisions that I do."

"Whenever you want to talk about it, I'll be ready to listen."

Sari appreciated him not pushing her for too much, too soon.

When it was time to get her boys home, Sari gathered up all their belongings and once again battled with herself about how to say goodbye to Damon. After a wonderful day together, she was so tempted to discover his kiss. She leaned in for a quick kiss to his cheek and he kissed hers in return, but she moved away before it could become more. Lingering close to him for too long was a bad idea, and it was not because she didn't trust him.

It was her own willpower in doubt.

Chapter Eight

Benjy and Jacob were playing on the rainbow-colored structure at the park when Sari spotted Damon walking toward her where she sat on a bench under an oak tree. They exchanged waves, and the butterflies—that only performed for him—started an acrobatic routine in her belly. She hadn't expected to see him today, but it was a nice surprise.

I shouldn't be this excited about someone I'm just "hanging out" with.

In black jeans and the white button-up shirt he always wore behind the bar, Damon looked so handsome. But then again, he looked good in everything. And no doubt even better without anything at all. With a jolt, the butterflies executed a daredevil trick on a flying trapeze.

For the love of chocolate. I need to stop this!

She could deny it all she wanted to others, but there was no more ignoring the glaring truth to herself. She'd been charmed and was falling for Damon. That was information she would keep to herself. She couldn't even tell Alana or Remi. Admitting it aloud would make it too real, and Mr. Casual had made his stance on serious or complicated relationships very clear.

They had an agreement. An understanding. They would hang out casually with no commitments. It's what she wanted. Under no circumstance could she let him know that her feelings were growing beyond their original agreement. The one *she* had suggested.

"How's it going, pretty lady?" He sat beside Sari and stretched his arm across the back of the bench to squeeze her shoulder.

Wanting him to know his touch was welcomed, she clasped her hand briefly over his. "Not bad at all. Are you headed to work?"

"Yep, but I'd rather be hanging out with you."

"Then you better hang on because I'm pretty exciting." She chuckled. "My wild evening consists of sitting on the playground watching my kids before going home to make dinner and then fall asleep soon after the boys do."

"You're more exciting than you realize." His hand moved to play with her long hair that was trailing over her shoulder. "Too bad we frequently work opposite shifts. I'm going in to work early so I have time to eat before my shift. I know you said it's hard to eat at a restaurant with little kids, but I also know you are tired. Come with me and we can wrangle the boys together while I buy you all dinner. I get an employee discount that I rarely use."

"You'd do that and risk wearing yourself out before your shift?"

"Bring it on, little mama."

Ordinarily she would hate it if a guy called her that, but when Damon said things like this, it made her smile. "In that case, I'm going to take you up on your offer, so I don't have to cook."

"Good." Benjy and Jacob spotted him, and he waved to them. "Think the boys are hungry yet?"

"I'm sure they are."

The kids ran their way, and Damon met them halfway. He picked up a boy under each arm and flew them over to the bench and set them at her feet. "Who wants to go eat dinner at the restaurant where I work?"

"I do," Benjy said.

"Me go, too." Jacob put his little hands on his chest.

"Yes, we're all going." She held out her hands to her kids and they started toward the parking area.

"I want to ride in Mr. Damon's race car," Benjy said.

"Sorry, but we won't all fit in his car. Mr. Damon

doesn't have a back seat." And she had no idea if he was a safe driver.

"I have a back seat," he said.

"One big enough for two car seats?"

He scratched his cheek. "Good point. I don't know about that."

Damon bent to Benjy's level. "Your mama is right. You need to be safe in your car seat. You ride in your car, and we can pretend we are on a secret mission. I'll watch out for the bad guys from the front, and you watch my back."

Why did this man have to be so great with her children? It was not helping with her falling-for- Damon problem.

When they got to their cars, she peered through the window into his tiny back seat. "Technically, that is a back seat, but it would be a challenge to wrangle their seating back there and get them strapped in tight."

"That's something I never thought about," he said.

And that was another reminder that he was a single guy with no plans to settle down anytime soon.

Once they got to the Chatelaine Bar and Grill, they chose one of the booths that was tucked into an alcove so it would be easier to keep the kids contained. They sat on the outer edges across from each other with Benjy on Damon's side and Jacob on hers.

A waitress with short red hair and lots of eye

makeup approached with menus. "Good evening. Damon, I thought you were working tonight."

"I am. Shift starts in less than an hour."

"Then we better not waste any time. What can I get everyone to drink?"

"Water for me and the boys," Sari said.

"Great. I'll be back in just a minute to take your order." She spun and hurried away.

Damon stared after her. "She didn't ask me what I wanted to drink."

"I guess she thinks you are one of the boys and want water, too." When Damon's eyes widened, she wanted to kick herself. The last thing she should be doing was freaking him out by being all possessive with him.

"I guess she does." His quick smile relieved some of her worries.

The waitress returned quickly, and they ordered while the kids colored on their paper menus. Their food arrived soon after and they were talking more about places he wanted to travel to when Damon tensed.

Sari followed his gaze, expecting to see another woman making eyes at him. "What's wrong?"

He and an older man exchanged a wave. "That's Martin Smith. He's the guy who was best friends with my late grandfather, Wendell Fortune, and the one who has given my brothers and my sister their inheritance checks. Every time I see him my heart jumps because I wonder if it's finally my turn."

"I can see how that would happen. I think I would do the exact same thing." She couldn't imagine what it would be like to know you had a huge payday coming. Sari brushed Jacob's hair back from his forehead, and when he smiled up at her with ketchup on his face, a burst of maternal love made her heart squeeze. There were so many more wonderful things about life than being rich. She glanced at Martin sitting at a table across the dining room. "It's odd that you didn't all get your money at the same time."

"It is strange. Apparently, my grandfather was an unusual man. But I'm learning to be patient," Damon said. "Waiting for my turn to collect my inheritance. And—" he dropped his voice to a whisper "—waiting for long, slow kisses."

His voice was pitched low for only her to hear, and it caressed her like a lover's touch. It was both playful and sexy, making her very impatient to try out the kind of kisses he was suggesting.

She brushed her fingertips over her lips. "I've heard that patience is often rewarded."

Damon was getting happily lost in Sari's blue eyes and the way she was smiling at him as she touched her plump pink lips, but the intense moment was cut short when Benjy put his ketchup-smeared hand on the cuff of Damon's white shirt.

"Oh, no." Sari gasped.

The little boy pulled his hand away and looked at his fingers. "Sorry."

"It's okay, kiddo. It'll wash out," he said.

She stood and leaned across the table to wipe her son's hands. "I was afraid something like this would happen."

"It's fine. I usually roll up my sleeves when I start working behind the bar." He stuck a napkin in his glass of water and washed off most of the ketchup.

"Since everyone is finished eating, I better get the boys home, and I don't want you to be late for your shift."

He looked at his watch. "I have just enough time to walk you out." He was tempted to hold her hand on the way to her car but had no idea how she felt about public displays of affection. On his way past the yellow rosebush by the door, he paused long enough to break off a flower.

Sari got the boys buckled in, turned on the car, got the air conditioner running and music playing, and then stood beside her open driver's door. "Thank you so much for dinner."

"You're welcome." Damon held out the flower, enjoying the flash of her pretty smile as she brought it to her nose and inhaled, and wanting so badly to close the last bit of distance between them. Close enough to connect with her lips. When she reached for his hand, he drew it to his mouth and kissed her knuckles.

"You know... I think dinner with my children has earned you at least another kiss on the cheek." Lifting onto her toes, she pressed her soft mouth to his cheek, her lips lingering a breath away from his. "But a flower deserves...more."

Her lips swept across his, soft as the brush of a feather, and it was the invitation he'd been hoping for. His kiss was meant to be brief, but one taste and he was captivated. He lingered long enough for her to moan, and they eased out of the kiss in a way that told him neither wanted to stop.

But they were in the parking lot. With her kids in the car. And he was about to be late for work.

Damn my timing.

But now he knew she was okay with at least some amount of public affection. "Can I take this as a sign that I can call you?"

"Yes. You may."

Her soft laugh was warm against his cheek, and unable to resist, he gave her one more quick kiss before stepping back.

"Maybe I shouldn't have kissed you in the parking lot of your workplace," she said.

"You won't hear me complaining."

She blushed and got into her car. "Good night."

"Drive safe." He bent so he could see the boys. "I'll see you two squirts tomorrow."

"Bye, Mr. Damon."

He waved as Sari and her boys drove away and then headed back inside the restaurant. He rolled up the sleeves of his shirt one more turn, which was thankfully enough to hide the child-sized ketchup handprint. The next time he had dinner with the kids, he'd have to remember to wait to put on his white work shirt until after the meal.

He was about to step behind the bar when someone called his name.

"Damon Fortune Maloney, I was hoping I'd seeing you here tonight."

The female voice was familiar, and he turned to see Katie, a woman he'd gone out with before she moved away. "Hi, Katie. It's good to see you."

She hugged him, and the way her hands roamed up and down his back and one slipped momentarily into his back pocket told him what she had on her mind. There was a time, not that long ago, he would have been right there with her. So…why wasn't he tempted to pull her into the back room for a long, hot kiss?

With a rush of heat to his chest, he knew the reason without giving it another second of thought. Sari Keeling. The beautiful woman who'd enchanted him.

He stepped back from Katie and moved behind the bar. "Have you moved back to town?"

"No, I'm only here to get the rest of my stuff, and I was hoping to run into you."

"Oh yeah? What's up?"

"My cousin was supposed to go to a concert with me in Austin on Friday night, but she can't go. And I know this is short notice, but my first thought was to ask you. I have a hotel room," she said in a quieter and suggestive tone.

Katie was a wild one—in and out of bed—and only a week ago he would have jumped at the chance to spend a weekend in a hotel with her. But instead of an enthusiastic hell yes, his brain fumbled for an excuse. An excuse! He had a rare Friday night off, but…he didn't want to go.

"I wish I could say yes. That would have been fun, but I can't get away that night." The disappointment was clear on her face, and he hated making any woman sad, but he couldn't say yes just to make her happy. "Rain check?"

"Absolutely. I'll be around for a few weeks packing the rest of my stuff."

He'd set himself up for that, and now he'd likely have to find another excuse in the coming days. "Tell your family hello for me."

"I will. I'll let you get to work." She went to join her family at a booth across the dining room.

While pouring beers, mixing margaritas and chatting with customers, he tried to tell himself all kinds of lies about why he'd declined Katie's invitation.

The truth was slapping him in the face. She wasn't Sari. Plain and simple. Because if it had been

Sari asking him to go away for a night together, he would've gone so far as to quit his job if he'd had to. But with Katie, a woman he'd once been crazy about, he'd made up an excuse that wasn't even true.

Well, shit.

His chest tightened and a touch of panic started to rattle behind his rib cage. He was in so much deeper than he was supposed to go with Sari.

How did this happen? And so quickly.

He and Sari had just shared a real kiss, and it had been stellar. There was something deeper than he usually felt developing between them. Something exciting, but also…scary.

He should walk over to Katie's table and accept the invitation if only to prove to himself that he wasn't getting in too deep with one woman. But he didn't. For the next few hours, he fought with himself about what to do. Sari was very clear about not wanting a committed, time-consuming relationship. He needed to get a grip and not let things spiral out of control.

In the morning, he would call…

One of them.

After a night of restless sleep, Damon had made a decision about his love life. He grabbed his phone from his nightstand and typed out a text message.

Good morning, beautiful. Give me a call when you have time.

Chapter Nine

The sweet sound of her children's laughter was the best way to start a morning. Sari was in the middle of making breakfast when her phone chimed with a text message. Fearing it was work asking her to come in early, she decided to ignore it until after they'd eaten, but when she glanced at the flower Damon had given her last night, warmth washed over her.

What if it's Damon?

Unable to resist, she put down the spatula and went over to the table to check her phone. Her stomach did a backflip. Damon wanted her to call him. She clapped her hands in that quick and quiet way people do when they are excited—or happened to be a thirteen-year-old girl.

"Are you happy, Mama?" Benjy asked from the living room couch. "You was dancin'."

She froze mid hip wiggle. *For the love of chocolate. I really am acting like a teenager.*

She blew a kiss to her son. "I am happy, sweetie."

It was a lightness. A sensation she hadn't felt in a couple of years. But there was still an echo of grief. Sari looked at her boys cuddled together. Jacob had his head resting on his big brother's lap and Benjy played with his little brother's hair.

It was okay for her to be happy again, right? She'd cried—a lot. She'd grieved. And she was ready for the fog of sadness to lift. Seth's greatest wish had been for his children to be happy. And she knew that extended to her. She thought back on the day a friend's husband told her he wouldn't want her to be with anyone else if he died. That had spurred a conversation with Seth, both of them agreeing that they would want the other to keep living and loving if something happened to one of them.

It was okay to stop feeling like she was doing something wrong by liking Damon, but that did not mean she was ready to dive right into a romantic relationship. But knowing what she did about his ability to "do casual," maybe he was the perfect man to help her dip her toes in the water. A guy who wasn't looking for more than a bit of fun wouldn't expect or even want more from her.

"Mama, sausage," Benjy yelled.

"Oh, shoot." She rushed back to the stove.

She'd call Damon in a little while. Right now, she had turkey sausage on the verge of burning and eggs that needed scrambling. Besides, it wouldn't do to seem too eager.

While she finished cooking, she tried to guess what he wanted to talk about. Did he just want to make small talk or was it something specific? He'd called her beautiful and added a winking emoji to his text message, so she was pretty sure it wasn't him saying he couldn't see her again.

Once the boys were fed and the dishes done, she sat on the arm of her red chair and dialed his number. Her foot tapped about five times for each ring.

"Hello. Damon's house, where the '70s never end," he said in a cheery tone.

She chuckled. "Good morning. Is that disco music I hear playing in the background?"

"Of course."

"Sorry it took me a few minutes to call you. I was cooking breakfast."

"No worries. I know your mornings are busy. Do you work today?"

"Yes. My shift starts in a few hours. What's up with you?"

"I have a question. If you can get babysitting, would you like to…hang out? Just the two of us?"

Her muscles twitched with the urge to dance again.

"I like the sound of that, but I have a couple of questions of my own. What time of the day?"

"Daytime into early evening, or however much of the evening you can get."

"What are we going to do?"

"It's a surprise."

She got the kind of flutter in her tummy that came along with a first crush. "Well… I at least need to know how I should dress."

"I'll be wearing shorts, a T-shirt and running shoes."

"Are we going jogging?" she said with a chuckle.

"No. It's much better than going for a run."

"Now you have me super curious. Can I have a hint?"

"Nope. But I do have one other question. Can you ride a bike?"

She laughed. "You're about as easy to get a secret out of as my boys. Yes, I can ride a bike."

"Oh, never fear. I still have a few surprises and tricks up my sleeve. You'll just have to wait for the full experience."

While waiting to hear back from Mrs. Mata about babysitting, Sari tried to focus on the romance novel she was reading, but all it was doing was making her think of Damon.

The way you could tell he was smiling just by looking at his eyes. The way his scent made her head swim in a most pleasant way. She pressed her fingertips to her lips, remembering their kiss. It hadn't been deep and lingering, but it held the promise of so much passion.

But she could not let daydreaming about him occupy too much of her time and get in the way of things she actually needed to be concentrating on. Like parenting and work.

On the day of her date with Damon, Sari took way more time than necessary getting ready for riding a bicycle. It didn't really call for makeup or her hair to be smoothed with a curling iron, but that didn't stop her from doing both. Stepping back from the mirror on her bedroom door, she checked her appearance one more time and was happy with her favorite khaki shorts, a turquoise T-shirt and the running shoes she picked up on a GreatStore sale rack with her employee discount.

She packed a tote bag with essentials and a few just-in-case items—since she wasn't totally sure of all he had planned. Thinking about Damon wanting to keep his date plans a surprise made her smile, but she was glad he'd told her to bring along a swimsuit. Since she couldn't decide which one was best, she packed three: a black-and-white one-piece, a red tankini that was fairly conservative and an emerald-green bikini that was on the sexy side. She would feel out the situation and then decide which one to put on when the time came.

Not wanting Benjy and Jacob to be upset that they were not included in the day's plans, she got the boys all set up with Mrs. Mata and then waited outside. The jittery, fun kind of nerves had her bouncing and ready for physical activity. She looked in her tote bag for the third time to make sure she had everything. Her swimsuits, hairbrush, mascara, sunscreen, a cover-up and a few healthy snacks since Damon would probably bring chips and candy.

His sleek silver car pulled into the parking lot of her apartment complex, and Sari slid into his passenger seat and resisted the temptation to lean across the console for a kiss. "Hi."

"You look beautiful, as always."

"Thank you." She turned to put her tote bag in the small back seat. "Where are the bikes?"

"They're at a friend's house at the lake. He's letting us borrow them." Damon pulled out onto the road. "He lives right by some nice biking trails, and since he and his wife are out of town, he offered us the use of his pool house and swimming pool to cool off after riding."

"How nice of him. That sounds great." She wondered again which swimsuit she'd reach for after spending time with him. They had skipped right over the kind of first dates where you go out for coffee or grabbed dinner. They had jumped into bets and dares that led to family dinners and spending the day at each other's homes. Now he had planned the kind of day that she enjoyed. Damon kept surprising her in all the best ways.

But he is young and about to be a rich man who will no doubt want to party and travel and...who knows what?

Damon turned down the volume on the radio. "How are Benjy and Jacob today?"

"Their usual busy-bee selves." She appreciated the way he thought about her kids. He knew she was a mom but had never made her feel like it was a problem.

"They weren't upset that you were leaving?"

"They were happy to have Mrs. Mata settled in for a Disney movie and then lunch and story time. But if they had seen you, there likely would have been some tears about us leaving them behind. They adore you." His smile was so genuine that it made something flutter in her chest.

"I'm pretty crazy about them, too. They must have a really great mom."

"Has anyone ever told you that you are a sweet-talker?"

"Who, me?"

The rest of the drive to Lake Chatelaine, they talked about music and concerts and favorite movies.

Damon drove down the long driveway of a huge

Tuscan-style home and parked around back in front of a three-car garage.

"Wow, this is some house. Who did you say lives here?"

"He's a surgeon. I coached his little boy's T-ball team. He asked me to check in on his house while they're in California."

He got out of the car and pulled a cooler from his trunk. "I brought some food and drinks. We can put them in the pool house refrigerator before we go for a ride. Unless you're hungry now?"

"I'm good with waiting. I brought a few snacks and water." She lifted her tote bag. "Mom habit, I guess."

"Always being prepared is a good thing in my book." He put down the cooler so he could unlock the door.

The two-bedroom pool house had high-end finishes and appliances and was bigger than her apartment and fancier than any home she'd ever lived in. The open-concept living, dining and kitchen area was decorated in shades of blue and tan. Tile flooring that looked like sun-bleached wood added to the beachy vibe of the space. "This is not what I pictured when you said pool house. This is more like a guesthouse."

"Or just someone's regular house." Damon put the cooler in the kitchen and then went back to the door to push a button that opened one of the garage doors.

"I'll get the bikes out. Will you put the food in the fridge, please?"

"Sure. I'll meet you outside in a few minutes." It was the first time she'd seen him in shorts, and she couldn't resist watching him as he walked across the parking area to the open garage on one end. His legs were tanned, long and leanly muscled like a runner.

Pulling her focus away from The Damon Show, she flipped open the lid of the cooler and was surprised to find somewhat healthy food options inside. Was this the kind of lunch he normally packed, or was it because of all her talk of eating right? She had a feeling it was the latter, and she couldn't help feeling a bit of pride that she was improving his eating habits. She got out hummus and carrots, pita bread, chicken salad and several kinds of fruit. No chips or candy anywhere in sight. But there was a small strawberry tart. There was also a bottle of cold white wine and a variety of other drink options, both alcoholic and nonalcoholic.

The day was warm, so Sari pulled her hair up into a high ponytail and went outside where Damon was checking the tire pressure on the bikes. "Are we all good to go?"

"Yes," he said. "The red bike is yours."

They biked along the smooth dirt trails that wound through wooded areas and occasionally came out into more open spaces closer to the water. In some spots the path was wide enough to ride side by side, and in others they took turns leading the way. They saw a few other people, but being a weekday, they had the trails mostly to themselves. Except for the wildlife. There were more deer than people and a few of them even darted across the trail.

She slowed her bike as another beautiful view of Lake Chatelaine appeared through the trees. "It's so pretty here. Can we stop and sit for a while?"

"We can stop anywhere you'd like." He leaned his bike against a tree next to hers, and they walked through a patch of yellow and orange wildflowers on their way to a big flat rock in the shade of a cypress tree. A pleasant breeze blew in from the water and cooled some of the sweat on her skin.

"This has been so fun, and now I want a bike," she said. "But the boys are so young, I'd have to get one of those bike trailers for them to ride in."

"The ones you can pull behind your bike?"

"Yes."

He picked a wildflower and tucked the stem into the hair tie holding her ponytail.

The brush of his arm against hers made her skin tingle. "I do have a double baby jogger I can push while running."

"Do you like to run?"

"I do." Sari picked up a smooth stone and skipped it across the water. "I used to go for a run several times a week. Lately, it's harder to find the time and energy. My baby jogger has space for two kids, but

Benjy is getting so big that his feet end up by Jacob's shoulders. And as you can imagine, that has caused a few problems along the way."

He chuckled. "I can see that being a problem. I can watch the boys if you ever want to go for a run, or if we go together, we can each push one. I bet they sell baby joggers at GreatStore."

"They do, but they aren't cheap."

His stomach growled. "I'm getting hungry. Are you ready to head back to the house?"

"Yes. I could go for some food myself."

As they were walking up from the water to where their bikes were leaning against a tree, Damon took her hand to help her up a steep area, and like he'd done before, he didn't let go. A moment later, he stopped and pointed off to the side. "Be very quiet," he whispered. "Look up in that big tree."

She was expecting to see a bird or squirrel and was very surprised to see a gray fox. The animal was flat on her tummy on a large branch with her muzzle resting on her white paws.

Sari smiled at Damon, and they stood very still. "I didn't know a fox could climb a tree," she whispered.

"They can. A gray fox has flexible rotating wrists and partially retractable claws. See the big knothole behind her? That's probably her den, and this time of year she might even have a few kits in there."

"How do you know all this?"

"I used to love reading about animals when I was a kid. Actually, I still do."

"You have that in common with Benjy and Jacob." She breathed in the fresh air and leaned her head on his shoulder, letting happiness and contentment soak in while she could. She'd been looking forward to this time alone with him and was having more fun than she had even anticipated.

They stood together watching the fox for several minutes, then once the animal lifted her head to look back, they got on their bikes and started toward the house. Since they weren't stopping to sightsee along the way, they rode harder and faster on the way back.

Sari flapped her T-shirt away from her skin. "I'm suddenly very thankful that you worked out a deal to use the pool."

"Do you want to jump in the water and cool off before we eat?" he asked.

"That sounds fabulous. And then we can eat at the outdoor table."

"Cool. I guess you'll want to wear a swimsuit?"

Her mind flashed straight to swimming naked, and she glanced to each side to check for close neighbors. "We can't skinny-dip in the broad daylight."

He started to speak but just grinned and then cleared his throat. "I didn't know that was an option, but I like the way you think, and I'd be happy to accommodate that one night soon."

She'd been hot before, but now her skin was flaming, and she put her hands to her cheeks. "Oh, you meant swimming in my clothes. Please, don't listen to me when I say stuff like that."

That certainly tells both of us where my *head is. What is wrong with me?*

He closed the distance between them and tucked a wisp of hair behind her ear. "Today, I want you to do and say and dress, or undress, any way you want. You deserve a day to be carefree."

"I'll try." She didn't bother saying that as a single mother she rarely let herself be completely carefree. She had been called high-strung a time or two. "Be back in a minute."

Sari took her tote bag into the pool house bathroom and glanced at herself in the mirror. "Way to go." After what she'd just said, she should probably put on her most conservative one-piece, but with a minute of consideration, she chose the small emerald-green bikini and tied a white sarong around her waist. Back outside, country music played on a sound system, and Damon's back was to her as he put food on the round table under a blue-striped umbrella.

He turned at the sound of her footsteps. "I think…" His words trailed off and he seemed to have lost the ability to speak.

His flattering reaction was worth her worry over which swimsuit to wear and made her feel both sexy and powerful. "You think what?"

"I have no idea. I forgot," he said with a chuckle

before jumping into the deep end of the pool as if he couldn't wait one more second to cool off.

She knew the feeling. Seeing him bare-chested in black swim trunks was making her own thoughts a bit scattered. She walked down the steps into the shallow end. The cool water surrounded her as she moved deeper. "This feels so wonderful. I haven't been swimming in a while. Seems like there are a lot of things I haven't been doing lately."

"I'm glad I can be the one to help you change that." He swam over but stopped just shy of touching her. "Do the boys know how to swim?"

"Benjy does, but I haven't had the opportunity to teach Jacob yet. But for safety reasons, I really should teach him soon."

"We can bring the boys over here one day, and I can help you."

When he suggested seeing her again, especially when he included her children in the plans, it made her swell with happiness that she knew was dangerous for her heart. "They would love that."

And so would I. A bit more than I should.

Chapter Ten

Guess I'm giving swimming lessons now.

Damon smoothed back his wet hair and took a deep breath in an effort to get a grip on his lust for Sari and the fear that he was getting too close to someone who didn't want a relationship. *He* was supposed to be the one who didn't want a relationship.

"Did you open the bottle of wine?" she asked.

"Yes. Let's eat and then get back in the water for a longer swim." He followed her up the steps in the shallow end. Her long wet hair glistened in the sunshine, trailing down to tease the small of her back, right where two dimples were visible above her bikini bottom.

He started to sit in the chair beside Sari but knew he'd struggle to keep his hands, and lips, off her.

Sitting across from her was the safest, if not his favorite, choice.

"Where is the place you'd most like to travel?" he asked.

"Ireland. What about you?"

"Ireland and Scotland are definitely on the list. Once I have my money, I plan to travel there and lots of other places."

"Tell me more about your plans," she said, and popped a raspberry into her mouth.

He swirled wine around in his plastic wineglass. "I'm thinking…swimming with dolphins in Hawaii, hiking in Peru to see Machu Picchu and someplace where the white water rafting is good."

"Those all sound very exciting and adventurous." She bit into a large strawberry, closed her eyes and made a sound that made him need to jump back into the water to cool off.

Currently, the most exciting thing he could think of was kissing the strawberry juice from her lips. And he'd only have to travel to the other side of the table.

With cold white wine in plastic glasses on the edge of the pool, they got back into the water. It felt natural to move into each other's arms. They swayed to the beat of the song on the radio, moving through the water like they were slow dancing.

"Thank you for hanging out with me today," he said.

"I should be the one thanking you. I haven't been able to relax like this in a long time."

"Glad to be of service." Her fingers played with the wet curls at the back of his head, and he shivered under her touch, drawing her body closer. Unable to hold out for one more millisecond, he brushed his lips against hers and was rewarded with her soft sigh. She opened to him, tasting of raspberries and something uniquely her.

Their kiss deepened and grew into a passionate exploration, water splashing between their bodies as they moved. His fingers slipped under the back tie of her bikini top, and he desperately wanted to pull the little string holding her top on, but he held on to enough control to stop himself.

Sari eased her head back just enough to meet his gaze. "Damon?' she whispered, her breath soft and sweet against his mouth.

He traced his fingers along the length of her back. "What do you need, honey?" She bit the corner of her lower lip, plump from his kisses, and he brushed his thumb over the spot to ease her tension into a smile. This whole day was about making her happy and giving her the mom break she needed. About making her smile in a way that fired something deep inside him.

"Tell me what you need and it's yours."

And heaven help him, he meant it.

"I don't know what I need."

"In this very moment, what is your greatest desire?" With their bodies pressed together, his desire was obvious.

"I'm feeling so many things all at once. I don't know where to begin."

"Take your time, honey. Just feel and enjoy whatever you desire."

The country music changed from a fast song to a ballad, and she smiled. "I love this song. Will you hold me close, just for a little while?"

"Absolutely." He'd hold her longer than a little while. With her cheek against his chest, they swayed to the beat of the music playing on the outdoor sound system. He'd never danced in the water before, but he liked it. The way the water caressed their skin and allowed them to slide against each other was so erotic.

Maybe I should put in a pool at my house once my money comes through.

Her hands slid up the length of his back to wrap around his shoulders. She wasn't dragging him to the closest bedroom, but he could feel the desire swelling between them. It was in the way she relaxed her weight against him. The way her fingers flexed and moved over the muscles along his back. And the way their hips brushed, leaving her with no doubt of the effect her touch was having on him.

They stayed that way for several songs before she inhaled deeply and raised her head. Her smile was more relaxed. "That was just what I needed. I haven't been held like that in a long time."

It was what he'd needed, too, and just hadn't known it. But that didn't keep him from hoping

she'd soon want to explore what more there was between them.

"I'm glad I won our game of darts," she said.

"I think we would have gotten to this moment
no matter which one of us won the game. At least
that was my hope from the first moment I saw you.
When you walked into the Chatelaine Bar and Grill
on ladies' night. You were walking between Remi
and Alana, but you stood out and I couldn't take my
eyes off you. It was a few more minutes before you
saw me for the first time."

"That's not exactly true. The first time I saw you
was at the bachelor auction in February."

"You were there?"

"I was. I wanted to bid on you, but you went for
way more money than I had to spend."

"I won't lie, I'm happy to hear that you wanted to
bid on me." He moved into deeper water until she
couldn't touch bottom, and just as he'd hoped, she
wrapped her legs around his waist.

She shivered in his arms. "If I remember correctly, you were one of the highest bids."

"Something like that." He'd been the top bid, but
bragging wasn't his thing. "I wish I had seen you
back then. But I see you now," he whispered against
her lips, then took her mouth in a deep kiss that he
felt in every part of his body.

All the while, he was making his way toward the
steps in the shallow end, and with his hands cradling

her butt, he carried her out of the pool with her still wrapped around his waist. When he stepped inside the pool house, she lowered her feet to the floor but didn't let go of him. They continued kissing with the front door wide open.

She put her hand against his cheek and slowly broke the kiss. "Damon, what are we doing?"

He had hoped they were going to bed, but if she wasn't as ready as him, it was not going to happen. There was no way in hell he would ever push a woman further than she wanted to go. "Only what you're comfortable with." At the moment, he was physically uncomfortable with his longing for this amazing woman.

"Neither of us wants a serious relationship right now. We discussed that at the very beginning."

"I remember." *And that plan sucks.*

"My boys are my focus, and I don't have that much more to give."

He'd keep his mouth shut and not tell her that he wanted to explore what there could be between them. She was very clear about her wishes. Pushing for more than she was ready for would risk her cutting him out of her life completely.

He'd never had to be this patient, but he'd also never wanted anyone this much.

What is going on with me?

"But maybe…" Sari twined her fingers in his hair. Hope spiked along with his pulse.

"Maybe we can—" An alarm sounded from her

phone on the poolside table, and she startled. "That's the timer I set to let us know when it's almost time to get home to the boys."

He let his hands slide down her arms to lace his fingers with hers. "Good thinking. It's easy to lose track of time when I'm with you."

"It sure is." She took a step back. "I'm going to go grab my phone and then change into my clothes." She left him standing alone beside the open door.

The day had gone by too fast. He wanted to hang on to this unfamiliar new feeling. And he really wanted to know what she'd been about to say before that damn alarm interrupted them.

But what he wanted most was... more. More Sari in his life. More time kissing and talking and laughing. Now he needed to find an opportunity to see if she'd finish her sentence. *Maybe we can...*

Maybe they could discuss a new plan.

Chapter Eleven

On the drive home from a date that was right up there with the very best of them, Sari relaxed into the leather passenger seat of Damon's car and let the built-in massager work its magic. The air conditioner cooled her skin, which was pink from the sun, and it was nice to have someone else driving.

Damon stopped at an intersection and smiled at her. "How are you doing over there?"

"Enjoying your fancy seat features and feeling relaxed and happy. Thank you for a wonderful day."

Her answer seemed to ease the tension he'd been carrying in his shoulders ever since her alarm ended their day together. What had he been thinking about over on his side of the car?

"I should be thanking you," he said. "You're lots of fun to hang out with."

"We can agree on that." She giggled then covered her mouth. "I mean that *you* are fun. I'm not calling myself fun."

"I think it's the combination of the two of us together that equals fun."

"You might be right."

And that was exactly what was adding an extra dose of difficulty to her self-discipline. It was too late to pretend that nothing was developing between them, but she'd always been good at setting her mind to something and sticking with it. If Damon only wanted casual fun until he set off on his travels, then she'd set her mind to that.

There was no contest that her kids were her number one priority. It was up to her and only her to raise her precious boys into good men like their daddy had been. Like Damon was. Her breath caught as her heart seemed to pause before giving an extra strong beat. That last thought startled her, and she cut a glance his way. He had a striking profile, and she could look at him all day, but for multiple reasons there was a limit on where things could go between them.

They were at different stages of life.

Sari admired the shape and form of his arm stretched out to adjust the radio. Having his arms wrapped around her in the pool had been a much-needed moment of therapy. Something she wouldn't mind repeating. Was there really a reason to deny herself this bit of happiness because of what would happen at a later date? In the here and now, Damon made her happy and helped her forget about some of her stress and worries, if only for a little while. If she was going to take care of her boys to the best of her ability, didn't she need to take care of herself, too?

He slid his hand across the console, faceup in invitation for her to take it. She laced her fingers with his and was rewarded with one of his brilliant, crooked smiles. He stroked her palm with his thumb, and just that small touch was enough to make a warm shiver ripple through her body.

It would suck to one day see him with someone else, but she'd dealt with much worse. And if she set her mind to it, she could enjoy time with Damon until he set out to tour the world. She had faith in herself that she was strong enough to deal with whatever came next.

Twenty minutes later, Damon pulled into an empty parking spot beside her dark blue Volvo and leaned across the console, hovering just out of kissing range. "I hate that our day is ending."

Sari made a split-second decision. "Then we should do something about that."

When Sari stepped through the front doorway of her apartment, Benjy and Jacob smiled, but when

Damon came in a few steps behind her, they jumped up and ran over for an enthusiastic greeting while Mrs. Mata waved from the kitchen.

"Mr. Damon, did you come to play with us?" Benjy asked.

Jacob clapped his tiny hands. "Day-me play?" The way Jacob said Damon's name was adorable.

"I came to hang out with all three of you."

Sari let the boys talk and walked into the kitchen. "Mrs. Mata, thank you so much for watching the boys today."

"Glad to give you a chance to get out and enjoy yourself. Your young man seems like a very nice fella." She gave Sari a quick one-armed side hug and smiled at Damon interacting with the boys.

"He is nice," Sari said with confidence.

"I'm going to get going and let y'all get on with your evening. Goodbye, *mijos,*" she said, and waved to the kids on her way to the door.

They called out their goodbyes, then went instantly back to questioning Damon about a random variety of topics.

"What should we do before it's time to eat dinner?" she asked.

Benjy grabbed both of her hands and leaned way back to swing from side to side while she supported his weight. "Wanna be a superhero, too, Mama?"

"Sure. What should my superhero name be?"

"Catwoman."

"I'm gonna go find my Batman costume." Benjy ran down the hallway and Jacob followed, leaving them alone in the living room.

Damon wrapped his arms around her waist and pulled her close. "When the boys aren't around, can I call you sexy cat?"

"You think I'm sexy?" With her hands roaming up and down his back, she nipped at his chin.

"Yes, ma'am. So sexy," Damon whispered in her ear.

Tingly shivers rippled across her skin, and she kissed him, tasting the peppermint candy he'd eaten in the car. "Will you wear your tinfoil wristbands? They are so hot."

"You know it. Let's get in there before they come looking for us."

"Mama. Are y'all coming?"

They both laughed and headed down the hallway.

A few hours later, Benjy and Jacob had been fed, bathed, read to by her and Damon, and they were finally asleep. Their romantic day had turned domestic, but they were back to just the two of them again.

The flickering glow from the TV was the only light in the living room as Sari sat next to Damon on the couch. When he raised an arm, she snuggled against his side, resting her head on his upper chest with her arm across his waist. It felt good to cuddle in the dark.

He started flipping through the channels looking for something to watch and stopped on a movie called *Bad Babysitter*.

"Do you think it means bad as in she kills people or bad as in naughty?" he asked.

"I'm not sure."

"When we first met, you said you were old enough to be my babysitter. What kind would you have been?"

"Probably a strict one who made you eat your vegetables."

"And what about now?" He twirled her hair around his finger. "What would you ask me to do?"

Tilting her head, she smiled at him. "Are you into role-playing?"

He chuckled and stroked his knuckles across her cheek. "I never have been, but there can always be a first time. I'm glad you wanted to extend our day."

"You are a really great hangout buddy."

He made a grumbly sound in his throat. "That makes it sound like you're one of my guy friends. And I don't kiss my buddies."

She laughed and traced a finger along his collarbone. "Do you want to be my special friend?"

Chapter Twelve

"Special friend? I like the sound of that."

Damon's senses were hyper aware of the woman in his arms. Her soft skin caressing his, the scent of peaches, and her beautiful smile a treat for his eyes.

Family dinner and putting kids to bed wasn't on Damon's usual date itinerary, but he'd enjoyed himself, and this adult time after the kids were asleep was something he could get used to. "Earlier, you were about to tell me something when your alarm interrupted you."

Sari tapped a finger against her lips. "Remind me what I said."

"You said, 'Maybe we can…'"

"I wasn't sure how to finish that sentence then or now. I guess the simplest answer is, let's take things one step at a time." As she spoke, her fingers teased the neck of his T-shirt, barely brushing his skin, but enough to make him shiver.

With Sari's arm draped across his chest and her warm body snuggled against him, he was unusually content, with no desire to jump up and go do anything, except take this woman to bed. But he'd promised not to push.

She nuzzled her lips against his neck. "Want to make out on the couch with your special friend before you go home?"

His whole body tingled at her suggestion. "You read my mind." Brushing her long hair back from her face, he kissed his way along her neck, easing her back onto the couch and bracing himself above her. "Sari, don't let me push you beyond what you're comfortable with. Show me what makes you happy."

Her grin bloomed into a full-watt smile. "Well, in that case, come closer and kiss me." She wrapped one leg around his hips and pulled him snug against her.

He was on fire for her and didn't leave the lady waiting. He kissed her long and deep, exploring and learning. With all the tenderness in him, he ran his hands along the curves of her body, searching for the places that made her arch and moan against his mouth. She was so sweet. So responsive. And even fully clothed, this experience was rocking his world.

How would he ever get enough of this woman?

Sari shifted, so eager to change positions and be

on top that they rolled right off the couch, his back hitting the floor with her landing on top of him.

"Oh, no." She was laughing as she cupped his cheek. "Are you okay?"

He was laughing too hard to answer, so he wrapped her in his arms and held her until they could catch their breath. Then they continued making out until he was able to pry himself away from her an hour later.

After a few hours of sleep, Damon was back at their apartment the next day. Today was the grand opening of Remi's Reads and they had promised Benjy they would take a ride in his car. He was glad he'd chosen the model with the back seat, but when he tried to strap in Jacob's car seat and Benjy's booster seat, it was a hell of a struggle, and didn't end up with stellar results. The seats tilted up on the outer sides and into each other in the center.

This was a learning experience, and now he knew why most family men often had big cars or trucks.

Sari came out of her front door with a backpack over her shoulder and a boy by each hand. "All ready to go?" she called to him.

"Well, I'll let you decide. Have a look."

She peered into the back. "Hmm."

"Day-me, up," Jacob said, and raised his arms.

"Come here, little buddy." Damon lifted him onto his hip. "You can say it. You told me so. This back seat is not suitable for two kids in car seats."

She kissed his cheek and then Jacob's. "It's not my style to gloat."

"Guess I should put them back into your car."

Benjy gasped. "No! I'm ridin' in the fancy race car."

"Are they hooked in tight?" she asked.

"I think so, but check it out and see what you think."

She folded the front passenger seat forward and wedged herself far enough in to test his work. "They're tight. Since we only have a short distance to go, it will be fine."

"Yay!" Benjy scrambled into the back as fast as he could before either adult had time to change their mind.

Once both boys were strapped in, it was even more obvious how their heads tilted toward each other.

"Mama, I'm crookied," Jacob said, and tried to straighten his body by leaning toward the window.

"I know you're crooked, sweetie. Can you make it a few minutes until we get to the bookstore party? We'll be out of the car in about five minutes."

"Okay."

"Go fast, Mr. Damon." Benjy made revving noises and kicked his feet.

Damon and Sari shared a smile, and he pulled out onto the road.

The former hardware store's old wooden building had been transformed into Remi's Reads in a way that retained a historic vibe. A grand opening banner hung across the front of the deep covered porch, and the wide double front doors were flanked by whiskey barrels of colorful flowers.

Sari carried Jacob, and Damon kept hold of Benjy's hand as they crossed the street. "It looks like a good turnout," he said.

"I knew it would be."

The bookstore was filled with family, friends and Chatelaine residents ready to celebrate the opening of a bookstore in their small town.

Waving to several people along the way, the four of them walked through the featured book displays up front and made their way to the back right corner.

"Mama, there's a tree *inside* the store," Benjy said, and let go of Damon's hand to head toward the children's section.

"I think that tree is the only reason he didn't spot the refreshment table," Sari whispered as they followed her son.

"How long do you think that will last?"

"Not long." She pointed a finger at Damon. "And before you ask, yes, I will let him eat something."

Damon pretended to zip his lips. He'd been wondering that exact thing but wisely kept that thought to himself.

The very realistic replica of an oak tree stretched up one corner to the ceiling, where branches fanned out and silk leaves dangled at different lengths. A

Lego table and a second table with some toys and games were centered on a brightly colored rug and surrounded by low bookshelves that gave easy access to children.

Jacob was still on Sari's hip, but Benjy scanned the space with wide eyes. "I can play with these toys? All of them?"

"Yes. But they have to stay in the kids' section on this pretty rug," she said.

"Down, Mama," Jacob said.

Damon spotted his brother Max and his fiancée Eliza across the store talking with another couple. "Do you see the guy in the blue T-shirt and the pretty woman in the red dress?"

Sari gazed in the direction he was pointing.

"That is my brother Max and his fiancée Eliza."

"She is the one who is a real estate agent?"

"Yes. Funny story about how they met. She was helping him buy a house, and he talked her into pretending they were a couple because the seller didn't want to sell his ranch to a single guy."

"And it worked?"

"It did. Now they really are a couple."

"I can't wait to meet them."

Damon caught sight of his mother coming in the front door. Now was a good time to introduce her to Sari.

Whoa...now I'm thinking about introducing her to Mom?

He never did that. Over the years, it was rare that any of them did.

He put a hand on the small of Sari's back. "Are you okay with meeting my mom? She just walked in."

"Of course." She worried her lower lip in a habit he'd learned meant she was nervous or overthinking.

He was about to tell her they didn't have to, but his mom spotted him and headed his way. Fingers crossed she wouldn't say anything that made him cringe. He waved to her as she drew close. "Hi, Mom."

She gave him a tight hug. "Damon, I guess it takes a party to be able to see you."

And there it was, the first statement out of her mouth was one meant to subtly guilt him about not coming to see her more often. "Guess we're all busy these days. I'd like for you to meet Sari Keeling."

"Nice to meet you. I'm Kimberly Maloney."

"It's great to finally meet you."

Kimberly's brows rose, and Damon knew she was wondering why Sari had heard about her, but not the other way around.

After a few minutes of small talk, someone called their mother up to the front of the store to see something, and Sari went into the kids' area to help the boys.

Damon made his way over and stood beside his three brothers, Linc, Max and Coop, at the refreshment table, but he couldn't stop sneaking glances at Sari playing with her children. Jacob toddled over to get the action figure Damon had in his pocket and then went racing back to his brother.

"Wow," Linc said with exaggerated wide eyes. "You've turned into a family man."

Damon rocked forward when Coop slapped him on the back. "Don't sweat it, bro. It happens to the best of us.

"Next, the kids will be calling you Daddy," Max chimed in with more teasing.

"Y'all need to shut it." Damon said under his breath, thankful Sari was far enough away not to hear them. "I don't want Sari to hear y'all talking like that. I don't want to freak her out when there's absolutely no reason."

All three of his older brothers laughed loud enough that several heads turned their way to see what was so funny.

"I'm serious," he hissed. "She is sensitive about stuff like that." He was not about to tell them how much time they'd been spending together.

Linc grabbed a chocolate cookie. "Whatever you say, baby brother. Keep telling yourself that and let us know how it works out for you." He took a bite as he made his way to Remi who was standing behind the front counter.

Coop and Max started talking about horses and walked away.

He and his brothers knew the pain and hardship of growing up without a father. Benjy and Jacob were going through the same thing, but they were starting to depend on him. Bond with him in a way he had longed for as a child. If they lost him...

Damon was sweating, and it wasn't because the room was hot. What about his big millionaire plans filled with travel and wining and dining lovely women in foreign locations? Living up the single life before even thinking about settling down? He was not looking to start an instant family. He was going against his own plan. Breaking his own rules.

He hadn't gone out with another woman since the night he'd met Sari at the Chatelaine Bar and Grill, and it was not because he hadn't had the opportunity. A couple of women had called and even more had come to see him at work, but he didn't ask any of them out, and when they suggested it, he always had an excuse because he didn't have the desire to spend time with anyone but Sari.

She was a single mom, and she did not want a serious relationship with him or anyone else and had outright stated that fact multiple times. She was not pushing for more with him or expressing her love. The blood was rushing in his ears, and he was scaring the hell out of himself. If he kept this up, he was going to end up being the one with the broken heart.

Maybe he should test himself and—

Before he could finish the thought about seeing anyone else, Sari turned her head and smiled at him, her crystal-blue eyes sparkling. Their gazes locked, and he tried to smile but it was difficult with his heart wedged somewhere near his throat, making breathing a challenge.

She tipped her head as if she could tell something was bothering him, but before she could come over to him, Alana pulled her back into conversation.

"Well, hell," he said under his breath.

His brothers were right. He could tell them all kinds of excuses and try all he wanted to fool the three of them, but he could no longer fool himself. Mr. Casual had met his match. There was no more denying that he had feelings for Sari. Real feelings that went beyond the casual fun he was comfortable with.

What is going on with me? Now what do I do?

The woman he was falling for had made it perfectly clear that she did not want a serious relationship.

Chapter Thirteen

Sari's chest tightened. Damon was attempting to smile at her from across the room, but his eyebrows were squished together, and his smile didn't match the top of his face. Only minutes before, he'd flashed a genuine smile, filled with affection, but now...

Something was wrong.

Was it something she'd said or done? Did his mother not like her? Before Sari could think too much more about it, a gorgeous woman with long, wavy blond hair stopped beside her.

"This is a great bookstore."

"It sure is," Sari said, returning her smile. While the woman scanned the room like she was looking for someone, Sari couldn't help admiring her glamorous sense of style. A gray pencil skirt and blue silk blouse gave her a classic elegance. She wasn't tall, but her black leather stilettos—which if Sari wasn't mistaken had red soles—gave her a boost of at least three to four inches. Her overall appearance spoke of wealth, and Sari was positive she had never seen her around town.

"It's a good turnout for such a small town," the woman said while tapping a silver pen on a leather-bound notebook.

The movement drew Sari's attention to her perfectly manicured nails, a high-gloss pale pink that glistened under the overhead lights. Her own nails had nothing more than a quick coat of clear polish she'd applied right before coming today. "Everyone is excited about Remi's Reads. It's the only place to buy books within miles. My kids are loving the children's section."

"At first, I thought that was a real tree. Do you know the owner?" She poised her pen on the paper as if ready to take notes, giving the impression she was a reporter here to do an interview or a story about the bookstore's grand opening.

"That's her behind the register. Remi Reynolds."

"I understand she is engaged to one of the Fortune Maloney brothers. Do you know which one?"

"Yes, to the oldest, Lincoln. He is the one beside her with the wavy dark-blond hair."

"And the others? Do you know all of Lincoln's siblings?"

"Most of them." What did the rest of them have to do with the bookstore's grand opening?

"Do you know how they came to find out that they're related to the Fortune family?"

Her questions had drifted way into territory that had nothing to do with the bookstore, and an uncomfortable sensation was settling in Sari's gut. This woman wasn't here to do a story on the opening of Remi's Reads. What if she wasn't a reporter at all? What if she was one of Damon's past lovers who had returned and was checking to see if he was rich or if he was engaged or married? Sari looked around for Damon and spotted him just in time to see him rushing out the front door. Had he seen them talking?

"I don't know anything about it."

Even though Sari knew the story about how Martin Smith found Justine in Rambling Rose, and then came to Chatelaine and started giving out fortunes to them one by one, she wasn't comfortable sharing any of this. She was about to ask the woman's name when Benjy called for her.

"Mama, there's brownies and cookies *and* cupcakes." Her son's eyes were as big around as the doughnuts as he headed for the table of treats.

"Excuse me. I need to check on my children." Jacob was safe on Mrs. Mata's lap in the story time rocking chair, so she rushed over to Benjy just as he was reaching for a cupcake with one hand and a brownie with the other. "Wait, son. Not both. You have to pick one."

His little mouth dropped open, and he looked at her like she had truly lost it.

She had to admit everything looked extremely tempting, and she had just told Damon that she would let Benjy eat something. "How about we get a few different things and then cut them into four pieces and that way all four of us can have a taste of different treats."

"Yes, yes, yes." He hopped from foot to foot. "Me, Jacob, you and Mr. Damon."

The hitch in her breath made her cough. She'd said *four* of them instead of three!

This combined with her unfounded jealousy while talking to the beautiful blonde was a sign that she needed to take another look at her relationship with Damon.

Benjy tugged her hand, pulling her out of her moment of panic. "Let's pick that and that and that, Mama." He handed her one of the clear plastic plates.

She selected a brownie, a vanilla cupcake with yellow frosting, a snickerdoodle cookie and a key lime square. She was about to go get Jacob when Damon came up beside her.

"Need some help?"

"Actually, yes. I'm having trouble controlling this little sugar monster and we haven't even eaten any cake yet."

He picked up the excited child and put him on his hip. "Hey, little dude, are you having fun?"

"Yes. There are toys and books and cupcakes and brownies and cookies," Benjy said.

"Damon, do you know that woman over—" Sari turned to point to where the gorgeous blonde had been standing, but she was gone. "Hmm. I don't know where she went, but she was asking lots of questions about you and your brothers and sister. It was kind of strange."

"Was she a reporter?"

As Benjy leaned in Damon's arms toward the plate in her hand, she broke off a piece of brownie and handed it to him. "I'm not sure. At first, I thought she was doing a story on Remi's Reads, but her questions veered off into territory that had nothing to do with the bookstore. It was kind of odd, so I didn't say much. Especially when she started asking about the inheritance your family members have been getting."

"That is weird. Tell me if you see her again." Damon seemed to have gotten over whatever was bothering him a few minutes ago.

"I thought maybe she was an old girlfriend of yours and that's why you rushed out the door."

He grinned and broke off his own bite of brownie. "I was helping an old couple get something out of the trunk of their car. Were you jealous?"

She waved a hand, doing her best to look casual.

"Of course not. Let's get Jacob and go eat this on the front porch so we don't make a mess."

Once the four of them were settled off to one side of the porch, Damon used a plastic knife to cut everything.

Benjy rocked from side to side with excitement. "Mr. Damon, Mama said we need four pieces. Family can share the same brownie, like we did at our house."

Oh my God.

Sari wanted to fade into the old wooden floorboards she was sitting on. She busied herself with tying Jacob's shoe because she couldn't look at Damon. If she didn't see a look of panic on his face, maybe she could convince herself that he hadn't notice her son's statement about family.

Chapter Fourteen

Sari had worked a morning shift at GreatStore, and they had arrived home just in time for the boys to take a nap. While they slept—and to occupy her mind from constantly thinking about Damon—she got her sewing machine from the back of her closet and set it up on the kitchen table.

She put the TV on a channel with romantic comedies and unfolded the red and blue fabric that she'd bought on the sale rack at work. After ironing it, she measured and cut out two blue and two red pieces that were just the right size for little superhero capes. For added safety, she made them with Velcro tabs at the neck so they would break away if the capes got caught on something. Or if one brother decided to

yank it off the other. Maybe she could even find superhero decals to iron onto the back.

The movie playing was about single parents, and
of course made her think of Damon. If he had noticed Benjy's "family" comment at the bookstore,
it hadn't seemed to bother him. After they'd come
home from Remi's Reads and she put the boys down
for a nap, their goodbye kiss had taken an hour and
almost made him late for work.

She looked at the fabric in her hands and got back
to thinking about what she was supposed to be doing.
This activity was not providing the distraction she'd
hoped, but an hour later, she had both capes made.

Benjy came into the kitchen as she was tidying
up her sewing supplies. "Hi, sweetie."

"What are you doing?" He came over to check
out the mess on the table.

"I'm sewing, and I made something for you and
your brother." She held up his cape, showing off the
reversible red and blue sides. "Will this be good for
when you play superhero?"

He smiled—looking so much like his father—and
bounced from foot to foot. "Put it on me, Mama."

She showed him the Velcro tabs and attached it
around his neck just as Jacob came into the room.

"Jacob, look. Mama made us super capes."

Her youngest rubbed his eyes, then came over
for a cuddle, not yet awake enough to appreciate
his new cape.

Benjy held out the material and spun around to test it. "Where is one for Mr. Damon?"

"You think he needs one too?" She went to the refrigerator for their snacks.

Her sweet son looked at her like that was one more in a long line of silly mom questions. "He has to have one. He's in our superhero club."

"Oh, of course. How silly of me." Would Damon think it was silly and be embarrassed to wear it? She smiled at the thought of the first day she'd caught him using a bedsheet as a cape, and knew he'd be okay with her making one for him.

"Make it right now, Mama."

"I don't think I heard the nice word."

"Please," he said. "Make it, make it, make it. Please, please, please." Like a pogo stick, he sprang into the air with each word.

She couldn't help laughing. "Let me see if I have enough fabric left."

"Can we go see Mr. Damon and play?"

"He's working this afternoon and evening, but I'll call him later and see what he's doing tomorrow or the next day."

Since the table was covered, Benjy helped her spread a plastic tablecloth on the kitchen floor for snack time. While the boys ate apples and almond butter, she unfolded the material to see if she had enough to make a cape for her six-foot-tall boyfriend. She gasped as her pulse tripped, then sped.

Boyfriend? Do I think of him as my boyfriend?

She groaned and covered her face. "Of course I do." Neither of them was going around town calling the other one their girlfriend or boyfriend, but apparently her brain hadn't been given the message. But talking to him about it…could ruin everything. Still, she wished he was here to talk to.

Her phone rang, startling her so much that she dropped a spool of thread. It rolled under the table, red thread trailing behind it. The photo she'd added for Damon's calls appeared on the screen. What were the chances of it being a coincidence that he'd called right when she wanted to talk to him?

She picked up the thread to give herself a few heartbeats and then answered. "Hi, Damon. Aren't you at work?"

"I'm on my break, but I have a question to ask you."

She also had a few questions, but ones she'd keep to herself for now. "Ask away."

"A customer gave me four passes to the San Antonio Zoo, and I thought you and the boys might like to go with me. Have you been there?"

"We have, but Jacob was so little he doesn't remember it. Benjy and Jacob will love that. I'm glad you called. The boys have a surprise for you and wanted me to find out when we might see you."

"Oh, yeah? Cool. I work a lunch shift tomorrow. I'd love to hang out in the evening."

His quick, enthusiastic reaction made her smile.

She'd frequently told him she didn't have more of herself to give because her boys were her focus, but was that really true, or just something she kept telling herself?

The following evening, they went over to Damon's. He was immediately presented with his cape by two excited little boys, and he did an excellent job of being appropriately enthusiastic.

He unfolded it to reveal the red-and-blue reversible cape. "This is so awesome."

"Mama made it," Benjy said.

"She did?" He grinned at Sari. "She's got lots of talents." He put it on and struck the Superman pose. "How's this?"

When her boys copied him, she used her phone to take their photo. She took more candid shots as they tested out their capes by zooming around his empty dining room. Damon's cape came down to the backs of his knees, and unfortunately hid the way his blue jeans hugged his cute backside.

"I have a surprise for you boys, too," Damon said. "Follow me." He opened the sliding glass door and they stepped outside. Just off the back patio was a green plastic sandbox shaped like a turtle. "My neighbor was giving it away, and I thought you two might like it."

"So cool," Benjy said.

Both little boys climbed in and started playing with the toys in the sand.

This handsome, in-demand single guy had put a sandbox in the backyard of his bachelor pad. Specifically for *her* kids. When he did things like this, he made it harder and harder for her to remember that words like *commitment* were not in the plan.

Many times, he'd mentioned his desire to travel, and once he got his Fortune money, there would be nothing stopping him. But traveling was something she could not do with him. She'd never be the party girl who could drop everything to get on a plane and fly away to somewhere exotic.

We're at different stages of life.

But they had right now, and she didn't want to give up seeing him. Unaware of her thoughts, Damon came up behind her and wrapped his arms around her waist. "I need help narrowing down my choices for remodeling materials. Will you and the boys go to the store with me sometime and help me pick things out and maybe get some samples? I need to get a better idea of the cost I'll be looking at."

"I'm happy to help, but are you sure you want all of us to go? You know it will come with a few challenges to have the kids with us, right?"

He kissed the side of her neck. "People do it all the time. If I call it a superhero mission and they wear their capes, it might even be fun."

"You really are just a big kid." She tipped her head back to smile at him.

"Told you I was."

"Oh, talking about shopping reminds me that I forgot to pick up a prescription." She turned to face him. "Can I leave the boys with you for about fifteen minutes while I go grab it?"

"Sure. We have some very important superhero business we need to tend to. Right, boys?"

Benjy gave a thumbs-up. "Right."

"Wight," Jacob said.

"You three be good. I'll be back soon."

"Bye-bye, Mama," Jacob said and waved a red shovel, flinging sand into the grass.

She blew kisses to her children. When Damon blew one to her, she pretended to snatch it from the air.

But what was really being snatched was her last shreds of willpower.

And her heart.

Damon couldn't resist watching Sari walk into his house, her long waves of red hair swinging across her back and teasing her curvy hips. His fingers tingled, and he flexed them, wanting so badly to touch her and explore her in a way he had not been able to yet. But he had a feeling they would get there.

With kids playing in his backyard and a woman he adored off running an errand, Damon felt… content. With only a touch of freaking out. More and

more he doubted his reasons for not wanting a serious relationship.

Sari frequently reminded him that she didn't
have that much of herself to give. But he was starting to seriously doubt that was true. Sari was filled
with love and kindness. And if his guess was correct, she'd been trying to convince herself that they
weren't in a real committed relationship just as much
as he had. They had both been fooling themselves.

Benjy held out the sides of his cape and jumped
off the patio, then performed a spin-and-kick maneu-
ver. "Do you think my daddy would've been good at
playing superhero?"

The question caught Damon off guard, but he answered quickly. "Absolutely. The very best."

He knew exactly what it was like to grow up without a father. And although he'd been so young—Jacob's age in fact—when his father left that he barely
remembered him, the effect of not having one around
to teach him things and help his mom had made an
impression on him. It had certainly made his mom
rigid, worn down and set in her ways. He didn't want
those same struggles for Benjy, Jacob or Sari.

*What would their father think of me and the way
I am connecting with his family?*

"Are there superheroes in heaven?" The four-year-
old wasn't done with the hard questions.

"I'm sure there are."

"Good. My daddy is in heaven. I hope he has a

cape, too." Benjy ran farther into the yard and around the big tree with the blue-and-red fabric flapping behind him.

Damon cleared his throat and wiped a tear from the corner of his eye. Children had a way of saying what was on their minds, and he decided he'd make more of an effort to listen and try to give these boys what he had not had while growing up.

He wasn't sure whether to mention this conversation to Sari. It might make her sad, but he had a feeling she would want to know what Benjy was thinking and feeling. They didn't really talk much about her husband, but maybe they should.

For the first time in his life, he was considering a truly committed long-term relationship.

Was he fooling himself that Sari wanted the same?

Chapter Fifteen

Sari stretched out her legs and leaned her back against the tree in Damon's backyard. The spring afternoon was warm and sunny. It was the kind of day that was perfect for being lazy, and she wished she had a hammock. If she mentioned that to Damon, he'd probably buy one.

While the boys played in the sandbox, Damon was laughing at something his brother said to him on the phone. Sari was a little envious of him having so much family. She had no siblings, and her parents—who had not planned on having kids—had been surprised by her arrival when her mother was forty-five and her father was fifty. Now both of them were gone.

Benjy ran over from the sandbox, plopped down

beside her and put his head on her lap. "Mama, we have to sleep here for Easter."

"We do? Why is that?"

He looked at her upside down and held both hands out with his palms up. "Because. Mr. Damon has more rooms."

She chuckled as she stroked his red hair back from his sweaty forehead. "So, you think that means the Easter Bunny will hide more eggs filled with candy?"

"Yes." He rolled over and jumped to his feet. "Let's practice tonight." Before she could say no or get up off the ground, he sprinted toward Damon while yelling, "We're sleeping here tonight!"

Damon's eyebrows rose comically high before his wide grin spread. "Is that right? Sounds like fun to me."

She hurried after her son. "Benjy Keeling, I did not say we are sleeping here."

"But, Mama," he said, dragging out her name in that way kids do when they are especially exasperated. "Why not?"

"We don't have pajamas or your toothbrushes or anything else with us." Not to mention, she knew she'd end up in bed with Damon the minute her kids went to sleep.

Her son sighed and put on an exaggerated frown. "No fair."

"We will talk about Easter and see if we can work something out."

Damon picked up the four-year-old and turned him upside down. "Look, now your frown is a smile."

Benjy squealed and giggled, and once Damon put him down, he ran off to join his little brother in the sandbox.

Damon put an arm around her waist and pulled her snug against his side. "I'm cool with you staying over. Anytime."

Sari bit her lip to keep from breaking into a huge smile or immediately saying yes. "You only have two beds."

"Correct. And that's a problem, why? Can't the boys share a bed?"

She returned his grin as she faced him and wrapped her arms around his neck. "Yes, but…"

He brushed his lips against her ear. "I'll share my bed with you."

His warm breath tickled her, and she shivered. "That could be dangerous."

He chuckled. "I don't bite…unless you ask me to."

When he playfully nipped at her earlobe, she kissed him, then rested her head on his chest and let him hold her, gently swaying to the sound of her children's chatter. The idea of sharing Damon's bed made her all shimmery inside and out. From the crown of her head to the tips of her toes.

She was not the kind of woman who had sex with a man without it meaning a lot more than a fun time. Plus, she was a mom and had to set a good example for her boys. If Benjy and Jacob knew she was sharing a bedroom with Damon, their relationship would feel like…

Love.

Her pulse rate suddenly picked up speed, and she lifted her head. "What would the boys think if they knew we shared a bed? You don't know what it's like to have to worry about the example you're setting for your kids."

"Not personally, but I do understand your concern. Sorry I was teasing you about it."

"It's okay. Honestly, a big part of it is that I know that if we stay over… I won't be able to resist."

He flashed her favorite crooked grin. "I knew you found me irresistible."

"And let's not forget cocky," she said with a laugh.

Jacob tried to throw an inflatable ball to Benjy, but it rolled their way. She picked it up and tossed it back to them.

Damon was more complex than she'd originally given him credit for. And so was their relationship. He was full of life and fun, but he wasn't only a good-time charmer. He was a good man. But could she count on him for the long haul?

"What was Benjy saying about Easter?" he asked.

"He wants to stay at your house for Easter, and he thought tonight would be a good practice run."

"Cool with me, but why does he want to stay here?"

"Because the bunny hides eggs in every room, and since you have more rooms in your house…"

He laughed. "He is a clever kid. He thinks more rooms will equal more candy?"

"Exactly. That kid is forever after sweets."

Damon sat on the edge of the picnic table. "Occasional treats or fast food are not the end of the world. You don't have to be the sugar police all the time."

Sari shot him a warning look, but he was looking at the boys and didn't see it.

He continued talking without seeing the expression on her face. "Let them eat like kids at least every now and then and he won't try to sneak sweets. It's okay to chill out a bit."

Her back stiffened. "Chill?"

Damon wished he was able to kick his own butt for having a mouth that too frequently got ahead of what good sense he possessed. Sari's expression and tone of voice told him he'd gone too far with his suggestions. He had gotten her revved up. It wasn't fury, but *happy* wasn't a word that came to mind either.

"Did you just tell me to chill out?"

"Uhm, did I say that?" He flashed his best *I'm sorry* smile.

With her hands on her hips and her eyebrows drawn into a vee, Sari took one deliberate step closer. "Damon, you don't know what the hell you are talking about."

He mimicked her movement and kissed the tip of her nose. "Is that right?" The fire in her eyes didn't deter him. It only made him want to kiss her more.

"I have my reasons for the way I feed my children and myself. Perfectly. Good. Reasons." The volume of her voice lowered dangerously. "I'm the only parent they have."

Damon's chest constricted. She was truly upset, and that's not at all what he had intended. He'd only wanted to have a healthy discussion and tease her about her strict food rules. "Honey, I'm so sorry. I'm a total bonehead. Please know that my teasing is only meant to be playful. Never to hurt you."

When he raised his arms to hug her, she put a hand on the center of his chest. "It's…" A tremble ran through her body. "It's still hard to talk about."

He placed his hand over hers, clasping it against his heart. "Please, forgive me. The last thing I meant to do was upset you or make you sad."

The tension left her body on her exhale. "I know. I'm just sensitive about the subject."

"You have every right to be. If you want to tell me about it, I'll do my best to understand, and try not to say anything else that requires putting another foot in my mouth. One boot is enough for the day."

That got a smile out of her before she rested her forehead on his chest above their hands. "I have to stay healthy and take care of them and keep them healthy, so they have a long and happy life."

When he was tempted to say more, he decided it was best to just shut up and listen.

"I guess it's fear of what can happen. And sorrow. I can't just snap my fingers and get over my husband's death."

"I can't imagine what you went through." This time when he opened his arms, she stepped into his embrace.

"For me, healing has been more like slowly turning on a dimmer switch. Maybe it would help if I told you what happened."

"Tell me. Please. I'd like to know you better."

"Seth was thirty-two, strong and healthy...or so we thought. But...he had a massive heart attack while he was mowing the grass."

He trailed his fingers through her long hair. That must be why she seemed unusually concerned the day he was mowing the grass and kept giving him water and telling him to take breaks. "How long ago was this?"

"It was just before Jacob was born."

"Oh, honey. You had to go through his birth alone?"

"Seth's father was with me. He's not in good health and lives with his brother in Amarillo. Also, my childhood best friend, Jessica, came from California, but without Seth, it was really hard."

"Let's sit while you tell me about it."

They sat in the shade of the tree, and she rested

her head on his shoulder. "As you can imagine, it was an extremely emotional day. Feeling my recent loss so acutely and instantly loving a precious new life was… It's hard to find the right words to express it." She looked up at Damon and caught him brushing a tear from his cheek.

"You felt Seth there with you?"

"Yes, I did." A few of her own tears fell, and he gently kissed them away.

She was opening up to him, and telling him more about it than she'd ever told anyone, and it felt good to share this with Damon.

Much to Damon's—and Benjy's—disappointment, they did not stay over at his house that night, but that didn't keep him from hoping it would happen in the near future. He waved to Sari and the boys as they drove away, then stood in his driveway for a few more minutes.

"I've lost my Mr. Casual status." A gust of wind blew his hair and seemed to be agreeing with that statement.

Of course he'd fallen for the first woman who wasn't trying to drag him into the bedroom. He understood Sari's reasons for keeping what she thought was a safe distance between them for the boys' sakes. And with this new information about her husband, he realized it was for her sake as well. She'd given birth to Jacob while mourning. Her heart was still fragile.

They needed more time alone to talk. Just the two of them. Because as much as they'd fought it, they were in a relationship. He rubbed a hand roughly through his hair and turned for his front door. He went straight to the kitchen and pulled a beer from the fridge and smiled as inspiration struck.

He had an idea that might solve the "sleeping over" problem.

Chapter Sixteen

Their work schedules kept them busy for the next couple of days, but that didn't stop them from talking on the phone two or sometimes three times a day.

Sari was packing the boys' bag for day care when her phone rang with the tune she'd programed for Damon's calls. With a smile, she answered. "Good morning."

"Hi, honey."

"What's up? I thought you might still be sleeping after working a late shift last night."

"I got a call to work a private lunchtime event on a boat at Lake Chatelaine. It's good money and I couldn't pass it up. Right now, I'm drinking coffee and trying to wake up, and I wanted to say good morning before you head in to work."

"I'm glad you did."

"I bought some new furniture," he said.

She held the phone against her ear with her shoulder while she added a couple of Jacob's Pull-Ups to the bag. "For the dining room?"

"For the blue room."

"Oh, that's great. I can't wait to see it." She resisted her urge to fuss at him for spending money and added a change of clothes for Jacob and zipped up the bag.

"How would you feel about going for a run with me after we get off work today?"

"I could use a run. I think the boys can handle a little while in the baby jogger."

"They might not have to."

"Damon, did you buy a baby jogger?"

"No, but I did arrange something. I hope I didn't overstep too much by doing this, but I saw your neighbor, Mrs. Mata, at the gas station yesterday and we got to talking. I asked if she could watch the boys for a few hours, and she said she'd be happy to because she wants to do an arts and craft project with them."

"You set up babysitting?"

"Are you mad?"

She chuckled. "No. But I am surprised. I have a feeling you've charmed Mrs. Mata just like you do every woman you meet."

"It's my superpower."

"I think we have found your perfect superhero

name. Captain Charming." Jacob started calling for her from the living room. "The boys are up to something, and I need to go. I'll call you when I get off work."

"Can't wait. Captain Charming, over and out."

"Bye." Sari finished the rest of her morning routine with a smile on her face.

When Mrs. Mata arrived to watch the boys, she'd gone on and on about how nice Damon was and said Sari needed to get out and about with her handsome young man. So now she was dressed for a run and headed to Damon's house. She wasn't even going to try to analyze why she was wearing a pretty pink bra and panty set under her running clothes.

Damon was coming out of his front door when she pulled into his driveway. "Sorry I'm a few minutes late." She wasn't going to tell him it was because she'd been touching up her makeup.

"It's perfect timing." He greeted her with a kiss. "Ready to run, or do you need to go inside?"

"Give me a second to stretch and then I'll be ready."

He moved into his own stretch. "I think we could both use this physical activity."

She could think of other physical activities she'd like to share with him. A few minutes later, they were headed toward a small neighborhood park with a trail that wound through a wooded area. They had only been jogging for about ten minutes when the sky darkened, and the first raindrops fell.

"Maybe I should have checked the weather," he said.

"I did check the weather, but there was only a ten percent chance of rain."

"Let's start back to the house."

The harder it rained the faster they ran. By the time they made it to the cover of Damon's front stoop, they were drenched, and she was shivering. He got the door open, and the chill of the air-conditioning made her even colder, and her teeth chattered.

"Good thing your front entry is tile," she said, and toed off her wet sneakers and socks.

"It can be slippery, so be careful. I'll go get towels." He peeled off his wet shirt and dropped it on top of his shoes.

Water droplets made lazy trails down the muscles of his bare chest, and she forgot what she was about to say. When his dripping jogging shorts came off next, he was standing before her in nothing but a pair of green boxer briefs. She went from chilled to burning up from the inside.

"Be right back." He walked carefully through the dining room and into his bedroom.

The view of his back and perfect butt in formfitting boxers was just as good as the front.

What am I waiting for? Why am I denying myself?

She didn't want to wait a moment longer. Not for

a towel and not to feel Damon against her, skin to skin. She stripped off her tank top and shorts but left on her bra and panties and then made her way to his room.

He was just coming out of his bathroom rubbing his head with one towel and holding another towel under his arm when she entered his bedroom. "Thought I'd just come to you."

He came to a sudden stop and his expression morphed quickly from surprise to a level of desire that rolled off him in waves. "Wow. You are such a beauty."

The appreciation in his brown eyes gave her the last bit of courage she needed. Feeling bold, she reached behind her back and unhooked her bra, holding his gaze as she let it fall to the floor. "Will you warm me up?"

"I… You…" He chuckled. "Coherent speech escapes me."

"Words can be overrated."

His towel fell to the floor as he opened the dry one and wrapped it around her, pulling her body snug against his. His skin was wet but warm, yet they shivered together upon contact.

Letting her hands roam and explore his chest, his back, his trim waist with sculpted abs was a delicious treat she'd been waiting for. Tipping her head back, she encouraged him to kiss her neck, and when she returned in kind, the rapid beat of his pulse thrummed against her lips.

His body told her that he was done with holding himself back every bit as much as she was. "Sari, honey." He tipped up her chin and held her gaze. The question was clear in his eyes as he gently stroked his thumb against her cheek. "Are you sure?"

"Yes. Please." Raising on her toes, she buried her hand in his hair and drew his mouth to hers. Their kiss was eager and full of passion and held a promise of things to come.

Still catching his breath after making love for the second time, Damon rose from the bed, gloriously naked and making her suddenly not so exhausted after all.

"Need anything?" he asked.

Sari stretched across the mattress. Her muscles were pleasantly sore. "Where are you going?"

"The kitchen. I need to refuel because somebody is a wild woman."

She giggled. "You're welcome. Bring the bowl of raspberries and a sparkling water, please." She hadn't felt this relaxed and sated in a long time. Making love to Damon had been worth the wait, but she was done with any more of that nonsense. Now that they knew how amazing they could be together, she was going to have a tough time staying out of his bed.

He returned with the berries and water and stretched out beside her.

"Damon, thank you for being patient with me. I imagine my pace has been slower than you're used to."

"You're not the kind of woman who has sex with a man just for fun. It has to mean something to you."

"You're very perceptive."

Damon kissed her softly before putting one plump raspberry in her mouth, then placed another in the hollow of her throat.

"What are you up to now?"

"You'll see." Stretched out beside her he propped up on one elbow and put another berry between her breasts, then another and another down the center of her body. A plump berry rested in her belly button, then another below that. He rose above her, kissed her softly, then ate the first berry.

Tender kisses and the warmth of his hands on her breasts made her breath speed. She was especially ticklish when he ate the one near her belly button, and laughing with him felt so good. She had been exhausted and ready to go to sleep, but Damon's attentions had reawakened her body, and apparently his, too.

"I thought you were exhausted," she said.

"I've been restored."

"From just a few raspberries?"

"From one taste of you." He touched the tip of his

tongue to the plumpest part of her full lower lip, and she responded by pushing him onto his back and taking charge of the moment.

The next afternoon when Damon didn't answer her knock, Sari let herself in his front door, and Benjy ran straight for the basket of toys. Jacob had fallen asleep in the car and was still on her hip trying to wake up. Music drifted from the back of the house, and she followed it to the kitchen. Damon was on his back with his head under the kitchen sink, an open toolbox at his feet. What was it about this scene that made him look so sexy and made her want to drag him to his feet and kiss him?

Jacob arched his back, and she set him on his feet. "Doing some plumbing?" she asked, loud enough to be heard over the country music.

Damon started at the sound of her voice, sat up too quickly and bumped his forehead on the top of the cabinet frame. "Shi… Ouch," he said, correcting his curse word as his eyes met Jacob's, and then he rubbed the center of his forehead.

"Sorry," she said, and clasped a hand over her mouth.

"Oh, no." Jacob toddled over, put his tiny hands on Damon's cheeks and kissed his forehead.

Sari's heart sighed with love. Her precious boy was so sweet. And Damon was so good with both of them.

"Thank you, little man. Now it's all better." He hugged the two-year-old and smiled at Sari.

She came close enough to give him a hand up off the floor. "I didn't mean to startle you."

"It's okay. I think we've established that I am a bonehead." With Jacob on one hip, he wrapped his free arm around her and gave her a chaste kiss. "I'm happy to see y'all."

Jacob leaned her way with his lips puckered, and she gave him a kiss, too.

"My mama," the little boy said, and patted her shoulder.

"That's right, sweetie. And Mama loves you so much."

Damon tickled the toddler's tummy, making him giggle before putting him on his feet. Jacob left the kitchen calling for his big brother.

Sari snuggled into his embrace, and they shared the kind of kiss that was reserved for private. She was getting lost in his taste and scent.

When they finally managed to pry their lips apart, she nodded toward the sink. "Plumbing problems?"

"No. I'm childproofing the house." He closed the cabinet door and demonstrated the lock he'd attached under the sink.

"You're doing this…for my boys?"

"If you're going to stay over for Easter, we can't have the little guys getting into stuff that's not good for them. And if I can get my sister's family to visit, it will be ready for her son, Morgan."

She swallowed the lump in her throat. Guys in casual relationships did not go to the trouble to childproof their houses, especially when it added the frustration of making it more difficult to open cabinets. Joy and excitement warred with caution.

The sandbox and now childproofing? What's next?

"There is one other thing. Go check out the blue room," he said.

"You have been busy." Sari went through the dining room to the back bedroom, expecting to see the retro hangout space they'd talked about. But she had not been prepared to see a pair of twin beds with a Spider-Man lamp on the nightstand between them.

This answered her "what's next" question.

"Now you can safely stay over for Easter."

His grin was on the mischievous side and *safe* was not the word that came to her mind. It sounded deliciously dangerous in the best ways.

"Damon, are you my boyfriend?" The words sprang out before she could stop them, and she pressed her fingers to her mouth.

What if he said no?

Chapter Seventeen

Damon's heart rate quickened. If someone had asked him a month ago if he'd want to call someone his girlfriend and not date anyone else, he would've laughed. But now there was nothing he wanted more.

"I sure hope I'm your boyfriend because you're my girlfriend."

"Really?"

He chuckled and wrapped his arms around her. "Yes, really. You sound so surprised."

"I'm…excited." She slid her fingers up the back of his neck and into his hair.

Her touch was tender but also spoke to him in a way words never could. "Good. I'm tired of pretending and trying to convince myself that we're not in a real relationship."

"Me, too. I can't believe you bought beds."

"Now everyone can have their own bed. And you can have your choice of beds."

"I like choices,"

"Mama, where are you?" Benjy called out from the hallway.

She stepped back from Damon. "We're in here."

He ran into the blue room followed by his little brother. "Is it time to go to the zoo?"

"No. Not until tomorrow morning."

"So, one more night?"

"Yes. One more night," she said, and sat on the foot of one of the beds.

Jacob climbed into her lap.

Benjy cocked his head, and his smile was a mile wide. "Hey, there's two beds. Mama, now we have to sleep here for Easter."

On the trip to San Antonio, Damon got the full experience of the Kidz Bop CD sung at top volume by a two- and four-year-old. And he was enjoying every minute of it.

"Welcome to my world," she said, and they shared a smile. "You might as well sing along."

Jacob fell asleep halfway through the drive, but Benjy was too excited and full of questions. Once they arrived, the kids were so wound up that he had to hold on to Benjy's hand so he would not run ahead of them.

"Should we rent one of the wagons?"

"Definitely," Sari said. "It will make the day much easier on all of us."

He rented a green one and a battery-powered fan that clipped onto the side. After swooping Jacob into the air and making him laugh, Damon then settled him into the wagon. "What animals should we go see first?"

"The bears," Benjy said, and climbed in behind his brother.

"Tiger," Jacob said, and let out his fiercest growl that made a passerby chuckle.

Sari unfolded the map. "First, let's look at this and plan the best way to make our way around the zoo."

Damon grinned but liked the way she always had a plan or was ready to make one. He wouldn't mind letting her put a few things in order in his life. His mother was going to appreciate the way Sari liked schedules and routines.

When they got to the primate area, the boys got out of the wagon. They spent a long time watching the orangutans because there was a new baby who delighted the boys. As they moved to other areas of the zoo, the kids wanted to take turns riding on Damon's shoulders.

They had chicken tenders for lunch, along with the baby carrots and cherry tomatoes she'd brought along in her bag.

Benjy stuck out his hands so Sari could clean

them with a wet wipe. "Mama, is this an ice cream day?"

"Yes, sweetie." She kissed his forehead. "Today is an ice cream day."

"Yay!" both boys cheered.

"Wow," Damon said, then chuckled when she punched his arm and shot him a playful glare.

"Something you'd like to say, Mr. Fortune Maloney?"

He wasn't foolish *all* the time and was a fairly quick learner. "Who wants chocolate and who wants vanilla?"

When everyone had an ice cream cone and the boys were situated in the wagon with a stack of napkins, Damon grabbed the handle and they started off toward the next area. "Hang on, boys."

The squawk and chirp of birds grew louder as they passed by the aviary. His chocolate cone was melting in the Texas heat, and he licked a drip sliding down his sugar cone before it could reach his fingers. Sari walked beside him, and he liked seeing her this carefree and relaxed and couldn't keep his eyes off her beautiful face, cheeks pink from the heat and sun.

"What?" she asked when she caught him staring. "Do I have something on my face?"

"No." He leaned over enough to kiss the corner of her mouth. "Just my lips."

"You look like you're thinking very hard about something."

"I probably shouldn't say what I was thinking."

"Now I have to know."

"Okay. But remember you asked for it." He kissed her once more, square on the mouth. "It's nice to see you relaxed and carefree."

"In other words, chilled out?" she asked.

"Exactly."

"Told you I'm not a total monster. This is a special day." She swirled her tongue around the top of her vanilla ice cream.

"You couldn't be a monster even if you tried." He agreed that it was a special day as well. It wasn't exactly the world travel he planned, but it was an adventure, and he could get used to days like this.

Benjy and Jacob had their little hands pressed to the glass of the lion habitat, completely enthralled with the prowling animals.

Sari shoved both of hers in the front pockets of her khaki shorts, reminding herself yet again not to cling to Damon like the baby orangutan who had made her boys giggle for five minutes straight. But resisting this tempting man was a challenge. He smiled at her and tingly flutters hit low and spread pleasantly through her body.

As if he could read her mind, Damon put his arm around her shoulders and kissed the side of her head.

Completely giving up on any level of resistance, she slipped her hands from her pockets and encircled his waist, enjoying the way the muscles of his back flexed under her touch.

"Having fun?" he asked her.

"I sure am." Being pressed against his leanly muscled body definitely fell into the lots of fun category.

An elderly couple stopped beside them. They were holding hands like young lovers, and Sari realized that being single and alone for the rest of her life sounded like the worst idea ever. She wanted to have a partner through all the ups and downs in the years ahead. Someone to hold her hand at graduations and at weddings and all the important stages of life.

"Your children are adorable," the woman said. "Our kids used to enjoy the zoo like your little ones."

"How many children do you have?" Sari asked.

"We have three. A boy and two girls." Her bright smile revealed a lifetime of happiness in the wrinkles around her blue eyes.

The man adjusted his baseball cap. "They have given us five grandchildren, and we have a great-grandbaby on the way."

"How wonderful. Congratulations." Sari hoped to be able to say something similar one day in the future.

Jacob turned from the lions and raised his arms to Damon, and he picked him up.

Benjy spun around and smiled up at the couple. "Where your kids at?"

"They aren't with us today," the man said. "But I used to bring them to the zoo just like your daddy does."

Sari bit the inside of her cheek to hold in her gasp. She wanted to look at Damon to judge his reaction at being mistaken for their father but couldn't make herself look directly at his face. Things were going so well, and she didn't want something like this to get in the way.

Benjy was too busy with questions and didn't seem to notice the use of the word *daddy*, but Jacob cocked his head and stared at Damon with a child's curiosity. He had never had anyone to call daddy. What was her toddler thinking?

"You just like the animals?" Benjy asked the man.

"That's right."

"Me, too." Her oldest—who was not shy like his little brother—turned back to the lions.

"Do your kids and grandkids live close?" Damon asked him.

"Most of them do."

The woman looked at her watch. "Sweetheart, we need to get going or we'll be late."

"Nice talking to y'all. You have a lovely family," the man said while looking at Damon.

This time Sari did cut a glance toward her boyfriend to judge his reaction to being mistaken for their father.

"Thank you," Damon said without correcting the man, but he rubbed the back of his neck.

By midafternoon, both little boys were asleep in the wagon, so they pulled it toward the front gate, hand in hand. They had to wake them up to return the wagon, and then the zoo exit sent them through one of the gift shops. While she followed her kids around to make sure they didn't get into any trouble, Damon went another direction. A few minutes later, he appeared beside them with a gift shop bag.

"What did you buy?" she asked.

"It's a surprise for later."

The ride home was not a loud singing ruckus like the trip to San Antonio had been. After one song, both of her tired little boys were napping in their car seats. She was tempted to talk to him about the man calling him daddy, but she chickened out. The day was too nice to risk messing it up.

Once they got back to her apartment, Damon helped her carry everything inside. Benjy and Jacob both had ice cream stains on their clothes and desperately needed a bath.

"Boys, tonight we are going to have a bath before dinner. You're sweaty and sticky, and you'll feel so much better after you're clean."

"I know the feeling," Damon said. "I am going

to run home for a shower and then if it's okay with you, bring back dinner from Harv's. And I promise not to bring brownies since they already had ice cream today."

"Maybe you are smarter than I thought," she teased, and kissed him. "That sounds perfect."

"I'll be back soon."

While he was gone, she bathed the boys and took a shower herself. She put on a red summer dress with spaghetti straps. It hit mid-thigh and made her feel pretty. When Damon returned, his reaction made her go from feeling pretty to feeling sexy.

After they ate, the boys went to sleep before it was even their bedtime. She and Damon collapsed onto her couch.

"Thanks for taking us to the zoo. Today was a lot of fun," she said.

"It was a great day." He stroked his fingers through her hair in a way that had become a habit they both enjoyed.

"There aren't many guys who want to take two small children on a daylong outing with a woman they haven't known for very long."

"I feel like I know you pretty well." He trailed his fingers slowly up her thigh, letting them slip under her skirt.

Sparks danced over every spot he touched. And she wanted his hands on every inch of her body.

"Do you get to know all the women in your life to this level?"

He flashed his crooked smile. "No. I can't say that I do."

"So…what's different about me?"

"So many things. For starters, you are a woman."

She laughed. "As opposed to what?"

"As opposed to a girl, like so many I've known and dated. You're mature and smart and funny and a wonderful loving mother."

"Thank you. I hope you see me as more than a mother."

"You know I do, honey." He slipped one of the straps off her shoulder and kissed a path from the curve of her neck to her lips.

"Want me to show you how *I* see you?"

"Yes." She sighed as his fingertips brushed the skin on her inner thigh. "Show me everything."

Damon was so turned on by Sari that he thought it couldn't get any better, but when she straddled his lap and tunneled her fingers into his hair, his body came more alive than he'd ever felt. Her touch was so addictive he couldn't imagine ever giving it up.

"I've known from the beginning that you're a charmer, but you're also so much more than I first expected."

"Tell me more." He grinned and pulled her hips closer.

"You kiss me in a way that makes me forget my troubles."

When she stopped biting her lip and smiled, he was ready to learn everything about her.

"And I like the way you so often make me smile," she said.

"Glad to hear it. You should smile all the time." He put his hands on her hips and pulled her snug against him, holding in a groan and loving her sweet sigh.

She ducked her head and brushed her lips softly against his, then took the kiss deeper.

She pulled back to look him in the eyes, and he brushed her long hair back from her pretty face. Looking at her like this, he realized he didn't want to do this with any other woman but her. "You're an amazing woman and mom."

"For tonight, can we just focus on the woman part?"

"Absolutely. Where would you like to do this…focusing?" When she gently tugged his lower lip with her teeth and her eyes flickered toward the hallway, his skin tingled, and his brain was screaming for more of this lovely woman.

"My bedroom."

Hell, yes.

That was the best thing he'd heard in ages. He grabbed the remote control from the armrest and turned off the TV, and they were bathed in darkness. Instead of letting her get up, he stood with her wrapped around his waist and walked down the short hallway. They paused at the boys' bedroom door and looked in on them before going into her room.

The door was barely closed before she grabbed the hem of his black T-shirt and yanked it up his body. He was more than eager to help and pulled it off, dropping it to the floor and then one at a time, he slipped the straps of her dress from her shoulders. The silky red fabric glided across her smooth skin, where it pooled at her feet.

Something about seeing their clothes side by side on her bedroom floor sparked an awareness. The depth of his feelings for her were staggering. And it felt so right.

With slow and deliberate movements, he caressed the curves of her hips, his fingers teasing under the lace edges of her black panties.

"Damon?" Her voice was a ragged whisper against his lips.

His whole body tingled as he slid one hand up to cradle the back of her head, and when she arched against him, he groaned. "Tell me what you need, honey. Let me grant your wish."

"Kiss me. Everywhere."

Chapter Eighteen

Sari's stomach gave a little leap like it always did whenever she first saw Damon. He was in his front yard as she and the boys pulled into his driveway to pick him up for their shopping trip to the home improvement store.

"Mama, roll my window," Benjy said.

She hit the button and watched her son in the rear-view mirror. Before the window was even halfway down, Benjy cupped his hands around his mouth. A sure sign he was about to yell.

"Mr. Damon, we brought our super capes," Benjy shouted from his booster seat, loud enough that Jacob covered his ears.

"Benjy, check your volume, please. That's too loud for inside a car."

"Sorry, Mama."

Damon strolled over in a sexy, leisurely fashion with his crooked smile that made her insides flutter.

He leaned in the open window to greet Benjy with a fist bump. "Howdy, kiddos."

"Day-me," Jacob said, and stuck his tiny hand out for his own fist bump.

"It sounds like you're ready for our important mission."

Benjy pointed to their capes that were tucked in the space between their seats. "Mama said we have to wait 'til we get there."

"She did?" He leaned in her open window for a quick kiss. "Hi, beautiful."

"Hi yourself, handsome. Hop in and I'll take you somewhere."

"Mr. Damon, where's your super cape?" Benjy asked. "You have to be a superhero, too."

Sari chuckled. "I don't think he wants to—"

"Of course I will," Damon said. "Let me run back in the house and grab it."

She watched her handsome boyfriend jog back to his front door. Sometimes she worried he might be too good to be true and at any moment something was going to go wrong and make this whole thing blow up in her face.

Damon settled onto the passenger seat and held up his cape. "I think your mom needs to make one of these for herself. What do you think, boys?"

"Pink one," Benjy said. "Mama likes pink."

"I can do that." Sari backed out of the driveway and was highly entertained by the three of them the whole drive.

At the home improvement store, she helped Jacob with his cape and settled him on her hip while Damon put his cape on, helped Benjy and then struck a pose that made her laugh.

"Hold Mr. Damon's hand in the parking lot, please." She got a big orange shopping cart, but neither kid wanted to get in it yet. Sari walked behind the three boys. With Damon between them, they walked hand in hand, sporting their matching capes. She couldn't resist pulling out her phone to take pictures of them. Other shoppers smiled, and Sari overheard several comments about what a good daddy Damon was or what a sweet family they made.

Sari pulled a small notebook out of her purse and wrote down prices and other pertinent information. They collected paint chips in a variety of colors, and took photos of flooring, cabinets, appliances and loads of other things.

Benjy fisted his hands on his hips and cocked his head, red hair falling over his forehead. "I been thinkin'. Since I know you good now, do I have to keep saying Mister? Can't I just say Damon?"

Damon's full-watt smile was an answer in itself, but he bent to her son's level and hugged him. "Sounds good to me, kiddo."

It was such a sweet scene, but a prickle of worry swirled in her gut.

Please don't let my relationship with him end up hurting my boys.

A few minutes later, Sari saw Martin Smith smiling at them, and they shared a wave. She did not point him out to Damon because she knew it made him anxious when he saw the man. It was having a similar effect on her, but for a different reason. Once he was a wealthy man, would it be the beginning of the end for their relationship?

He dreamed of traveling to faraway exotic places that she couldn't follow, and saddling him with an instant family would be taking away his dream. That had the potential to lead to future problems. What she and Damon had together was beautiful but her young boyfriend was originally only meant to be a temporary part of their lives. Lately, she'd let herself forget that. It had already gone on longer and become far more serious than she'd ever imagined.

"Mama, we're waiting for you," Benjy called to her.

"Oh, sorry." She caught up to the boys at the end of the carpet aisle. She'd been standing there staring into space while her thoughts took her on a roller coaster.

Having people once again mistake Damon as their father and seeing Martin had kicked up the worry she kept tucked in a corner of her mind. Something she'd been ignoring because she was having so much fun with Damon. But as a mother, she needed to make sure she protected her children.

One and a half hours of shopping was all the kids could handle without having a meltdown. They'd bought ten small bottles of paint samples to try out around his house, and they had managed to make a lot of decisions and had a long list of options to choose from.

Back to Damon's house, Sari put on an episode of Benjy and Jacob's favorite cartoon, and they watched while also zooming their toy cars across the bricks in front of the fireplace. She and Damon painted several swatches in most of the rooms, and after they dried, they walked from room to room picking their favorites. Sari liked the pale silvery gray in Damon's bedroom and a mossy shade of green for the living room walls. The last room they considered was the kitchen. She sat at the table and stared at the wall but couldn't chose among the three shades of blue.

Damon stood in front of the refrigerator and rubbed his stomach. "I'm hungry. I think it's time I start on the burgers for dinner." He also had salad makings to make Sari happy. And he had to agree that eating healthy was a pretty good thing.

Sari glanced at the clock and then jumped up from her seat at the table. "Oh, no. Look at the time. We blew right past naptime." She paced back and forth. "This is bad. A day at the zoo was one thing, but I can't let the boys get off schedule on regular days."

Damon bent to grab a couple of cold drinks from the fridge. "You shouldn't be so rigid with your schedule." When he stood and held out one of the sparkling waters she liked, her expression was an instant clue that he'd put his foot in it again.

Her eyes narrowed in a way that was chillier than the bottle in his hand. "Is my rigidity on top of me needing to chill out?" Before he could respond, her expression suddenly shifted to one of concern. "Do you really think that about me? That I'm too rigid?"

He grimaced and put the drinks on the counter. "No, I do not think you are too rigid. That came out wrong. I think we've established that I don't always choose my words carefully enough before they come out of my fool mouth." He really needed to work on that "brain to mouth without any thought" thing. "I said it because it's something I don't want to happen to you."

This time her eyebrows rose, and she drummed her fingers on her crossed arms. "I think you better explain further."

His gut clenched. Upsetting Sari was the worst. "I was thinking of my mother when I said it. I don't want you to become worn down and jaded by life the way she has been."

"Oh." Her shoulders relaxed. "What do you mean?"

"You became a single mom because of tragic circumstances. My mom had a husband who chose to leave her with four small boys and a baby on the way. He left her. Left us."

"Damon, that's terrible." She came forward and put her hands on his shoulders, and he gripped her hips.

"He never even met Justine, and I barely remember him. But I do remember how it was for my mom while I was growing up. She had to work very hard to support and take care of five rowdy children all on her own. Kimberly Maloney is very set in her ways and has trouble adjusting if her routine gets upset. I don't want that to happen to you."

"I can appreciate the fact that you're trying to look out for me, but I can't just throw our schedule out the window. Young children need routine."

"You're right. I shouldn't try to give advice about stuff I don't know about yet."

"You might not know all the kid stuff, but I think you do know something about what life can be like for a single mom. And… I suppose I could stand to be less sensitive about things."

He let his hands slide up and down her arms. "Honey, you are rockin' this motherhood thing. Please don't *ever* let me make you doubt that. You amaze me every day."

"Well, we might have missed nap time, but let's get dinner started before we get the boys even more off their schedule."

Damon flipped the hamburger patties on his backyard grill and watched the kids play. All day, he'd taken special note of the remodeling materials that made Sari's eyes light up... Just in case. Were they headed for a relationship that would eventually involve living in the same house? Was he ready to be a family man? A full-time father? A wave of chill bumps covered his skin.

Is that what I want?

What about his big millionaire plans? Traveling. Single women around the world. Adventures. All the single-guy stuff. Spoiling himself with things he'd never been able to have. But now he wanted to spoil Sari, Benjy and Jacob. And the thought of getting on a plane and leaving them behind made his stomach hurt.

Since the moment he'd seen Sari walk into the Chatelaine Bar and Grill on ladies' night, he had not had the desire to be with another woman. She was an unexpected but wonderful surprise. And so were her little boys. Were his brothers right about what they'd said at the grand opening of Remi's Reads?

He flipped the burgers and watched Sari and the boys kicking a big red ball around his backyard. She locked eyes with him and smiled in a way that made the tension in his chest loosen and fade away.

The only thing missing was a pet.

Chapter Nineteen

Damon's house wasn't new—by fifty years—but the wooden toolshed in his backyard had been added not long before he bought the place. He opened the double doors and pulled out the lawn mower, edger and blower.

"I've got a lot of extra space in here."

Raising his arms above his head, he laid his palms flat against the ceiling. One of the many home renovation videos he'd recently been watching sprang to mind. A family had turned a toolshed much like his into a pink and frilly playhouse for their little girls, but he had a different slant on the idea, and it was so much better than storage space for lawn mowers and yard tools. He had room for all those things in his two-car garage. This shed would make a perfect superhero clubhouse. "This could be fun."

He could fix it up for not too much money. His credit card still had room on it, and Martin had promised his money would come along...eventually. He abandoned the yard work idea and moved everything to the garage. Now that the shed was empty, he swept and got rid of cobwebs and dust, and it was ready for a makeover.

After a trip to the home improvement store, he painted the ceiling and top half of the walls sky blue and the bottom half of the walls dark blue. When the paint was dry, he covered the floor with a red-and-white outdoor rug. He thought about going to Great-Store to buy things to fill it up, but that ran the risk of someone questioning him about his purchases, or since Sari was at work, her catching him in the act. And he wanted it to be a surprise. Instead, he got on his computer and ordered a few things. He bought a little kid-sized table and chairs, a play kitchen with plastic food and dishes, and a couple of laminated superhero-themed posters.

A few days later, he was ready to reveal what he'd done with the shed. He had country music playing when Sari and the boys came in the front door.

Jacob ran to him with his arms raised. "Day-me, up."

"There's my little buddy." He lifted him high into the air before bringing him in for a hug.

"We brought food," Benjy said, and held up a plastic container. "I don't know what it is, but Mama said it's not cake."

He got his hugs and kisses from all three of them. "Boys, can you help me in the backyard? I have a surprise."

"A 'prise for me?" Benjy asked while tugging on Damon's shirt and bouncing on his toes.

"Yes. For you and your brother and me, too."

Sari smiled but with a tilt to her head that he'd learned meant she was concerned. "What did you buy now?"

"I only fixed up something I already had." They all four went into the backyard to the shed.

Benjy turned in a circle. "Where is it? I don't see anything new."

"Inside this shed. Should we open it?"

"Yes," the boys said in unison.

Damon unlatched the double doors and swung them open wide, and both boys rushed forward with wide eyes.

"Wow. So awesome," Benjy yelled, but since they were outside, Sari didn't correct him.

The boys went inside to inspect their new playhouse while Damon pushed each door back flush with the shed and held them open with large hooks to keep the door from blowing shut or any little fingers getting smashed.

Sari stepped into the clubhouse. "When did you do this?"

"Over the last few days."

"You really should not be spending your money on us. Especially money you don't have yet."

"I didn't spend that much."

But his purchases had been adding up. She wasn't wrong about that. If his money didn't arrive soon, he was going to max out his credit card.

A few days later, Sari and the kids met Damon for dinner at the Chatelaine Bar and Grill after she got off work. But as soon as her workday ended, his was starting. He was now behind the bar and ready to start his shift.

With a little boy by each hand, she leaned across the bar to give Damon a quick goodbye kiss. "We'll see you tomorrow evening?"

"Yes, you will. Boys, take care of your mama."

"Okay. We will," Benjy said with a big smile and a thumbs up.

Sari turned to go and that's when she saw Martin Smith in one of the tucked-away booths that was closest to the bar. This man was everywhere. Was he keeping an eye on Damon? Did it have something to do with when he would get his money? He waved, and because she had a child by each hand, she smiled and nodded. She glanced over her shoulder at Damon, wondering if he'd spotted the man who literally held his silver mine fortune in his hands.

Seeing Martin was always a reminder that Damon would soon be a rich man. His world would change overnight.

"Mama, do we have to go to day care tomorrow?" Benjy asked as she buckled his seat belt.

"Yes, sweetie. I work a morning shift."

"Oh, man. Bummer. When will you stop going to work, Mama?"

She sighed and started the car. "I'm afraid I'll have to keep going to work. But pretty soon you'll be in school and won't have to go to day care."

And then Jacob will be alone at day care.

Her stomach clenched, making her wish she hadn't eaten so much.

The thought of being wealthy and not having to work while someone else looked after her kids was appealing, but every time her mind even thought about drifting in that direction, she put an immediate halt to those daydreams. She'd rather live simply or even struggle than end up in a relationship where Damon someday resented being with them because he missed out on his big adventures. It could end up ruining their relationship, and heaven forbid they married and ended up divorced.

It wasn't only herself she had to think about. Money was not enough to risk all four of their hearts.

It wasn't just talk when she told Damon she was

an independent woman and liked to do things on her own. She was on track to move into management, and then she could put aside extra money and start taking online classes to finish her accounting degree. While Damon's goal was traveling and experiencing adventures, this was hers. A degree, a good job and being the best mother she could be.

She just didn't want to be lonely while doing it. But was that possible?

The restaurant was slow this evening, and Damon was bored, and watching the minutes tick by on the clock wasn't helping his shift move along any faster. The real root of the problem was that he'd waved goodbye to Sari and the boys, wishing he was going home with them instead of working a night shift. Because he was here serving drinks, he would miss story time before the kids went to bed. He'd miss cuddling with Sari on the couch as they watched TV. And he'd miss the feeling of being part of a family.

One of the waitresses came up to the bar. "Can I get a glass of chardonnay and one of merlot, please?"

"Coming up," he said, and prepared the drink order.

"Are you having a bad night?" she asked as she put the glasses on her tray.

"No, just tired." It was more than that, but she didn't need to hear about it.

"I hear that. I could use a vacation," she said before walking away.

He wasn't just tired. He used to love his bartending job, but that's when he was more of a night owl and could sleep as late as he wanted. Now there were things to get up for. Bartending was no longer a good fit for his life. But he had to pay the bills until his inheritance came through.

With a sigh, he poured himself a Coke, took a long sip and then rubbed his tired eyes.

"Hi, Damon."

He looked up and smiled at the woman who had sold him his silver car. "Hey, Mary. Good to see you. What can I get for you this evening?"

"I'd like a glass of cabernet sauvignon, please. How are you enjoying your new car?"

"I love it, but I've been meaning to give you a call."

"Oh, really? What's up?" She sat on one of the empty barstools. "Tell me."

He poured wine into a glass and put it in front of her. "I want to find out how much I'll lose if I trade in my car."

Her brow furrowed. "Is it because your money hasn't come as soon as you thought it would?"

"No, it's not that. Well…not just that. When I bought it, I never envisioned needing to put car seats in it."

"Car seats?" She said in a voice that was a bit too

loud, and several people looked their way. "Now I really need to hear more." She sipped her wine and propped an elbow on the bar top, giving him her full attention.

"I've been dating a woman who has two little boys." A genuine smile pulled at his lips the way it often did when thinking of Sari and the boys.

"Is it the pretty redhead who I passed on my way in?"

"That's her," he said proudly.

"And you're dating her exclusively?"

"Yes." When her eyes widened, he chuckled.

"I thought I'd noticed a few women distressed over you seemingly being out of the dating pool."

"No way."

"I'm not kidding." She tucked her blond hair behind her ear. "So many sad women out there."

"You exaggerate."

She laughed and took another sip. "Not so much."

Now that he really thought about it, he had made a lot of excuses lately to get out of invitations with women. He glanced around as if one of them might appear at any moment.

"So, back to the car," Mary said. "What are you thinking you want instead?"

"I want a car that is safe and more suited to driving kids around."

"So, a family car."

I can't believe I'm doing this.

She smiled as if she could read his mind. "I have several cars that I think you might like. And you might be in luck because I have someone looking for one exactly like yours. Since you haven't had it long, I think I can talk them into buying a gently used car."

"That would be great. Can I come by the dealership tomorrow morning?"

"Sure. I'll be there." She patted his hand. "I'm happy for you, Damon." She took her drink and went to join her party seated at a booth across the restaurant.

After filling a large drink order, Damon knocked over a glass of ice and sighed when he had to bend down to clean it up. The scrape of a barstool scooting on the floor alerted him to someone taking a seat at the bar. He stood to see Martin Smith grinning at him.

Damon's stomach did a backflip. Was today the day he would become a millionaire? Could he quit this job and do something with a regular schedule?

Be cool.

"Evening, Martin. What can I get for you?"

"I'll have the eighteen-year single malt scotch on the rocks, please. Just don't tell my doctor." He propped his crossed forearms on the bar top. "What's been going on with you lately? Still seeing the pretty one with the kids?"

Was the whole town talking about him dating Sari? "Yes, sir."

"Thought I'd give you an update. There's still a bit more red tape to clear up before your money is released, but it shouldn't be long now."

A wave of heaviness settled into his body. "Waiting is certainly teaching me patience." He set the drink in front of Martin.

"It can do that, or sometimes just make you want to pull your hair out."

Damon chuckled and actually was tempted to tug at his hair. He did love his fancy convertible, but he loved Sari and the boys more than any car.

Did I just say love?

The following evening, Damon got a text from Sari that she was swinging by and he went outside when he heard her pull into his driveway. When he got to the driver's-side door, she was rolling down the windows before turning off the car, and she put a finger to her lips.

"Both boys fell asleep," she whispered.

Once she got out, he leaned in for a kiss. "Hi, honey. I'm happy for the unexpected visit."

"Instead of going straight home from work, I wanted to bring over the folding chairs you wanted from GreatStore. They went on sale today and were going fast, so I grabbed a few."

"Thank you. Let me know what I owe you."

"Who else is here?" she asked, and pointed to his maroon Toyota SUV.

"No one. It's just me."

"Then whose 4Runner is this?"

"That would be my new vehicle."

She gasped. "Damon Fortune Maloney, you bought a second car?"

He chuckled. "No. I traded in my impractical car for this one. It's used, but in great condition."

"Really? You actually traded it in? I thought you loved your sports car."

He shrugged. "This one is pretty cool, too. It's four-wheel drive."

"*Why* did you trade in your car?"

He'd planned to tell her the real reason, but the way she was looking at him gave him pause. He didn't want her overthinking things. "Lower car payments. Come check it out. There's lots of space."

Sari glanced in the back seat to make sure the boys were still sleeping and then took his hand as they walked around the front of her car to check out his new ride.

"It's a great color," she said. "And look at that. It's got an actual back seat."

"Benjy is probably going to be sad that the race car is gone, but at least now I can take us places, so you don't always have to drive."

With her hand sliding under the front of his shirt, she gave him a sexy smile. "Want to drive it over to my apartment…and hang out with me after the boys go to bed?"

"Do we get to hang out in your bed?"

"That can definitely be arranged."

"Let me unload the chairs and get my keys."

Chapter Twenty

Damon's wonky doorbell rang, and he swore he'd replace it in the next few days. He answered to find Martin Smith, and as usual, his breath got lodged somewhere on its way to his lungs.

"Hi, Damon. Can I come inside?"

"Of course. Let's go sit in the kitchen. Want some coffee? I just made a pot."

"I'd love a cup."

Was Martin just here to torture him with anticipation? He was starting to worry that Linc had jinxed him when he said his money might never come. Red tape—whatever that entailed—was holding up his check. And if he didn't get it soon, he'd look into learning about the legal ins and outs of all this.

"How do you take your coffee?"

"Black, please. What happened to your silver sports car?" Martin asked as he took a seat at Damon's wobbly table.

"I traded it in. I needed something with a bigger back seat and good safety rating."

"Does it have anything to do with your pretty girl's cute little kids I've seen you with around town?"

Damon couldn't hold back the smile. "It does. An SUV is better suited to driving around toddlers with car seats and all their gear."

Martin chuckled. "Since I've been in Chatelaine, I've watched you change."

"In good ways, I hope?"

"Yes. You seem to have grown up." He pulled a white envelope from his shirt pocket. "This is for you."

Damon's pulse was tripping over itself, and he forced his hand not to shake as he took it. "Is this..." He cleared his throat, afraid to jinx it by saying the words.

"Open it, son."

Damon slid his finger under the back flap of the envelope and pulled out a check with a whole lot of zeros. "Wow." His adrenaline spiked, making his heart race. "Thank you so much Martin."

Was it a coincidence that his money was coming right after he'd traded in his car? He realized he didn't care because it was more important to him to have a safe car no matter how much money he had in the bank. He had loved that sports car, but he loved Sari and the boys more.

I just said love.

"Are you still breathing, son?" Martin asked with a gravelly chuckle.

Damon took an extra deep breath just to be sure. "Yep, still breathing."

"I know there were a lot of delays getting this money to you, but now you can go ahead and remodel your house and buy something nice for your girl and her boys."

"How'd you know I'm remodeling my house? Other than the fact that you can tell it needs it just by looking around this kitchen."

"I saw you at the home improvement store shopping with the kids."

After they shared a cup of coffee and more conversation that Damon barely remembered, Martin left, but promised to come back for a housewarming party.

Everything felt surreal. He'd thought after watching his siblings become wealthy one by one that he knew what to expect, but it had only been a guess. It was as scary as it was exciting. He wanted to do everything all at once. Pay off his house and car. Shop. Go on a trip. Buy gifts—mainly for Sari , Benjy and Jacob. But first, he needed to get this check to the bank and get some financial advice. And then figure out what he wanted to do with his life, because he couldn't just sit around doing nothing.

Instead of calling Sari straightaway, he decided it would be better to tell her in person, with gifts.

He didn't want to take his eyes off the check while he got dressed, just in case it blew away or got wet or somehow disappeared and he discovered he was still asleep and this was all a dream. At the bank, he asked if they could go into one of the offices to talk. Everyone would eventually discover he got his money, but it didn't have to be today.

Next, he went to the Chatelaine Bar and Grill to talk to the manager about quitting his job but promised not to leave them shorthanded if they needed him to work a few more shifts. After a few text messages with Sari, he was set to go over to her apartment in a few hours. Shopping was next on the list. He bought toys for the boys and a necklace with an emerald pendant. The color would be gorgeous with Sari's red hair.

Sari had just turned off the water in the shower when one of the boys started knocking on the bathroom door.

"Mama," Benjy yelled. "We got a present for you."

She put on her floral-print robe, grabbed a towel for her hair and stepped out of the steamy bathroom with a smile, expecting to see a handmade drawing or pipe cleaner sculpture. She did not expect to see

Damon standing there, but it was a lovely surprise that made her whole body tingle.

"I have news." Damon's smile was full-watt and had spilled over to excite Benjy and Jacob, turning them into bouncy little boys.

With her wet hair dripping down her back, she put the towel around her shoulders. "Don't make me wait. Tell me."

"I had to open a new bank account," Damon said.

She pressed her hands to her cheeks. "You got your money?"

"I sure did."

"And we all got a present," Benjy said, and started pulling her into the living room.

They hadn't been kidding. There were new toys and books on the coffee table and Jacob handed her a small box.

"For me?"

"Yep," Benjy said. "Sorry you didn't get a toy, Mama."

Damon chuckled and tousled Benjy's red hair. "I think she'll like this better."

The box was square and too flat to be a ring box, but when she opened it, she still sucked in a shocked breath. A very beautiful emerald necklace gleamed on black velvet. The brilliantly cut jewel was encircled with tiny diamonds and hanging from a gold chain. "Damon, this is too much."

"No, it's not. You deserve so much more than

jewelry, but I thought it would look nice with your red hair."

"I love it. Thank you so much." Sari kissed him and couldn't believe he'd bought something so extravagant for her, but with Damon, it was always an exciting ride.

But now that he was a wealthy man, how much longer would this ride last?

Chapter Twenty-One

The day before Easter, Sari packed a bag for the boys and herself, which was an unusual thing. She packed their day care bag almost every day, but an overnight bag was different. Other than going to visit Seth's father a few times a year, they didn't go many places that required a suitcase.

For herself, she added a pair of pink pajamas with a fitted top and shorts. Then like she'd done with the swimsuits, she tossed in a couple more options. A pale green nightshirt that hit mid-thigh and a longer silky spaghetti-strap nightgown that hugged her curves. She wasn't sure who was more excited about sleeping at his house, her or the boys.

Pull yourself together, girl. There has never been

any talk of forever. She'd been having to remind herself of this more frequently as of late.

She put all the Easter goodies in a blue plastic container and hid it in the back of her car right before they were ready to drive over to Damon's house. Then she loaded up the kids and away they went for an overnight adventure.

When they got there, Benjy rushed ahead of her and Jacob. "We're here," he yelled as soon as he had Damon's front door open.

Sari sighed but chuckled and caught up to him. "Stop yelling, son."

"Okay," he said in a voice that was almost as loud.

Damon was laughing as he stood in the doorway to the kitchen. "Do you have a lot to bring inside?"

"Only some furniture and dishes," she said, but couldn't hold a straight face.

He met her in the center of the still-empty dining room for a kiss. "You joke, but those are both things I could use. This big old house is pretty empty." He walked ahead of her to the car. "It can get lonely. There are a few things I'd like to add to my home."

Without being able to see his face, she couldn't judge his expression, and she paused to scold herself for hoping for thing she shouldn't. She could *not* start picturing herself and her boys living in this house with him.

But…was he hinting at wanting more between them?

From the front seat, she got the cartons of eggs. "I brought two dozen eggs that are already boiled and ready to dye," she said as they went back inside.

"That sounds fun."

"Did you dye eggs with your family when you were a kid?"

"Sometimes. When my mom wasn't too busy."

Sari put the boys' things in the blue bedroom with the new twin beds and her bag in the other guest room, even though she knew she'd spend a portion of the night in Damon's room.

In Damon's bed.

She shivered. Damon always left her apartment before morning, but tomorrow, they'd wake up in their pajamas and have coffee together. And watch her children hunt for Easter eggs.

They had fun dyeing Easter eggs at Damon's kitchen table. Jacob ended up with a blue hand, and Benjy broke an egg when he got overexcited and it flew out of his hand to land on the floor. Damon picked it up, peeled it and ate it, making the boys giggle.

With the excitement of the Easter Bunny's impending visit, it was more of a challenge than usual to get the boys to sleep. Once it was finally accomplished, she pulled the bedroom door almost closed, and they tiptoed away.

After they were sure the boys were sound asleep, she got out the tub of Easter candy and plastic eggs that needed to be filled. She was surprised to see that Damon had also bought stuff for the boys' Easter baskets.

They hid the colorful plastic eggs all over the house. They even sneaked a few into the room where the boys were sleeping and put eggs in their shoes. Beside each bed they put an Easter basket with a chocolate bunny, a sprinkle of candy and the stuffed animals Damon had bought. A purple stuffed cat for Jacob and a black cat for Benjy.

"Are you tired?" she asked him.

"No. I'm ready to spend some alone time with you."

That was just what she was hoping for. "Can we spend it in your bedroom?"

He swooped her up into his arms so fast that she squealed. "Yes, ma'am, I can't think of anything I'd rather do."

"I could go for a shower before bed," she whispered in his ear.

"I stand corrected. I'd like to do that first." He carried her into the master bedroom.

"Wait. I need my bag with my pajamas in it."

"Honey, you won't be needing those anytime soon."

When the boys woke up at six o'clock in the morning, Sari had to pry her eyes open because she hadn't exactly gotten much sleep. But every minute of the night before had been worth it. In a short time, Damon had learned what she liked and found the places on her body that made her come alive. They were more than good together in the bedroom.

The boys were thrilled with their Easter baskets and stuffed cats, and they went from room to room finding eggs.

Jacob shook his cat in front of his big brother's face as if to tell him that there were in fact purple cats. "Purpur cat."

"It's not real," Benjy said.

Sari knew Benjy had been sneaking candy all morning but decided to let it go for today. She was trying to take Damon's suggestions and chill out a bit.

She had encouraged Damon to invite his family over because she said he was lucky to have so much family around. They were in the backyard getting things ready for the potluck lunch when Benjy came over and sat beside Damon on the edge of the patio.

"What's wrong, kiddo?"

The little boy looked up at him with an expression Sari recognized, but before she could shout a warning, Benjy leaned over and threw up directly onto Damon's lap.

"Oh, shoot," Sari said, and rushed over.

Damon was frozen in place and appeared to be holding his breath.

She grabbed the roll of paper towels from the

picnic table and knelt beside them. "Are you okay, sweetie?"

"Unsure," Damon said, then looked up from his lap. "But you weren't talking to me, were you?"

"Not exactly."

"I'm okay," Benjy said and let her wipe his mouth. "I feel better now."

"I think somebody ate too much candy." She didn't feel the need to explain to Damon that this was one of the reasons she had rules about food. He had received the message loud and clear, with added visual and odiferous effects.

Thankfully this had happened in the backyard and not in the house, so with a water hose, cleanup was a bit easier. And he had time to shower and change his clothes before his family members got here.

Coop and Alana arrived first with fried chicken followed by Linc and Remi with beans and dessert. Max and Eliza came in next with a dish of macaroni and cheese, and his mother was the last to arrive with loads more food.

Most of the family was in the backyard, but Alana was in the kitchen helping Sari gather the last few things that needed to be brought out to the folding tables under the tree.

"Your maternity dress is adorable." It was pastel blue with pink cherry blossoms, perfect for Easter.

"Thanks. Coop brought it home to me yesterday."

Alana put both hands on her stomach and smiled. "Come feel the baby kicking."

Sari put a hand on the mound of her friend's baby bump, startled by a sudden longing to once again experience this for herself. "I loved this part of being pregnant. Actually, I loved all of it once I was past the morning sickness."

"Don't I know it. I was so glad when that stage was over." Alana turned and pulled a bowl of potato salad out of the refrigerator and put it on the countertop by the sink. "I can't believe this old refrigerator still runs."

"Right? It came with the house, but it's a bit of an eyesore and makes some interesting noises."

"Damon obviously hasn't been going wild with his money."

"Not yet. Other than trying to spoil my children." *And me.* She touched the gorgeous emerald pendant resting against her breastbone and then added more ice to the lemonade. "Now that he has the money, the refrigerator is getting replaced this week. I told him not to buy the most expensive model just because he could."

"Good advice." She gave Sari an assessing look. "You really aren't motivated by money, are you?"

Sari shrugged and continued stirring the lemonade. "Not really. I've learned that there are other things in life that are so much more important.

Money really can't buy happiness or fix problems." *Or bring back loved ones.*

"I need a serving spoon," Alana said.

"In the drawer by the sink," Sari said from the pantry. She heard several drawers open and close, then looked over her shoulder. "The other side of the sink."

"Are you and Damon going on a trip?"

"No. Why do you ask?"

Alana held up a handful of travel brochures. "These were in one of the drawers. Sorry, I'm being nosy. I'll put them back."

Putting them back couldn't take away the painful knot in Sari's chest. It wasn't like this was a surprise because she'd known all along about his plans. But that didn't make it any easier. Would this be the start of them drifting apart?

"Are you okay?"

Sari put on the best smile she could. There was no reason to ruin today worrying about that now. "Just tired. Damon and I didn't get much sleep last night," she said in a whisper.

Alana grinned. "As it should be. Tell me about the renovations Damon plans to do in here."

Sari heard the grinding shudder of the sliding glass door—one more thing that needed replacing— as someone came inside the house, but she didn't think much about it.

"Now that the money is in the bank, the cabinet

doors are being replaced by white Shaker style. A big apron-front sink. An island with storage underneath. Of course, new flooring, paint and all new appliances."

"What about the countertops?"

"Granite or marble."

"That all sounds very expensive," someone said behind them.

Sari spun around to see Damon's mom, Kimberly, standing in the kitchen doorway with her arms crossed over her chest and a tilt to her head that suggested she had a few thoughts on the matter. Sari's mouth went dry, and she swallowed hard. "Kitchens and bathrooms can be expensive, but I'm trying to help him find the best deals."

Alana picked up the potato salad. "I better get this outside."

Sari wanted to tell her friend not to leave her alone with his mother, but she stayed brave. "Can I get anything for you or help you find something?"

"No thank you." Kimberly went to the sink to wash her hands. "You seem to know this kitchen pretty well. I suppose going from an apartment to a big house is nice."

Sari's stomach suddenly felt like Benjy's had earlier. "Oh, the boys and I don't live here. We're only visiting like you are." Well, maybe not quite like that, but still… It's not like they were moving in.

"What can I help you carry outside?" Kimberly asked.

"I'll bring the lemonade if you'll grab that stack of cups."

Sari followed the sound of her children's chatter over to the clubhouse, but she stopped when she heard Damon's brother Max asking about the little white building.

"Bro, did you do this because you're starting a day care or something?"

"No. Don't you remember the clubhouse we used to have?"

"That fell down a long time ago, and it wasn't near this nice," Max said.

"I know. That's why I made this one. Now my nieces and nephews will have somewhere to play when I have backyard barbecues."

"Not to mention—" Max stopped talking when he spotted Sari.

She had a feeling he'd been about to say something about her children, who were currently pretending to cook their own meal at the toy stove.

"It's time to eat," she said.

Everyone took seats around folding tables that were lined up in the shade of the big tree. The conversation was lively, and everyone was laughing at a story Eliza was telling about the house she'd been showing to prospective buyers when they found someone asleep in one of the bedrooms.

During a lull in the conversation, Benjy started telling everyone about sleeping in the blue room. "Mama, we need to move to this house," Benjy announced to everyone in the backyard.

Sari froze and wished she could quietly slip under the table.

Chapter Twenty-Two

Damon had just finished ordering building materials and scheduling tradespeople to start on the renovations when his stomach growled. It was a bit early for lunch, but he was hungry. He briefly thought about eating a salad like Sari would, but quickly shelved that idea and got out makings for grilled cheese. He turned up the music on the radio because a silent house made him edgy. Growing up being one of five kids, he wasn't used to so much quiet. When Sari and the boys were here, the house was filled with life and love.

It was thoughts like this that kept leading him back to what Benjy had said at their family Easter lunch about moving into his house. It had momentarily freaked him out, but that feeling had faded.

Now he couldn't stop thinking about what it would be like to have them living here. Was it a scary prospect? Definitely. He knew Sari enough to know she was probably more freaked out than him.

He put his grilled cheese sandwich in the hot skillet and poured a glass of iced tea. One night soon, they needed to talk and figure out how closely their thoughts aligned. Since she was jumpy about the subject of serious relationships, it might be best if the kids were not just one room away while they talked.

"We need another date."

He could plan a special evening and tell her the things he'd been holding in. While he ate, he flipped through possible date ideas. This was the first time he was able to plan a date and not have money be an issue.

Sari was off work tomorrow night, but before he asked her out, he decided to first see if he could set up babysitting. With one phone call, he tentatively had Alana and Coop scheduled. Next, he called Sari.

"Hello."

Hearing her voice made him smile. "Hi, honey. Are you on your way to work yet?" He was so amped up he couldn't sit still and paced around his house.

"I just got the boys settled at day care and I'm about to clock in. What's up?"

"Would you be okay with Alana and Coop watching the boys for a few hours tomorrow night so I can take you on a date? Coop said they could watch them at your apartment."

"I'd like that. Where are we going?"

"Somewhere that we won't be wearing running gear. A dress would be more appropriate."

"And that's all the information you're going to give me, isn't it?"

He chuckled. "That's right."

"You like surprising me, don't you?"

"Yes, ma'am. I sure do." How surprised was she going to be when he confessed his feelings?

Sari was stocking shelves in the baking aisle of GreatStore when someone called her name. She turned and almost dropped a bag of marshmallows when she saw Damon's mother. "Hi, Kimberly. How are you?"

"I'm good. Just picking up a few things. I enjoyed watching Benjy and Jacob having so much fun on Easter. They're sweet little boys."

"Thank you. I have to agree with you." Sari relaxed a bit. Maybe she didn't need to be so nervous around Kimberly after all.

"But… I couldn't help noticing how attached they are to Damon."

Sari's mere second of calm vanished. She swallowed against the knot of tension that was growing in her throat, and she tried not to completely squash the bag of marshmallows in her hand. "He's good with them."

"I can tell he really likes you and the kids."

"We like him, too. You raised an amazing son."

"Thank you." Kimberly grabbed a bag of chocolate chips and put them into her shopping cart. "I just wanted to say, single mom to single mom, that you should be careful. Damon has never been one to stick with any one thing for long. I don't want you or your little ones getting hurt."

"I see." *What the hell am I supposed to say to that?*

"I'm certainly not telling you not to date him. Just to be cautious and plan ahead."

Sari was good at planning ahead, usually. But this thing with Damon had rapidly spiraled out of her control. Her heart was listening about as well as her toddlers when she said it was bedtime. "I'll keep that in mind." Which was not at all what she really wanted to say to a woman who was laying out some of her biggest fears. And this on top of the travel brochures was really getting in her head.

"I'll let you get back to work. Hope I see you again soon," Kimberly said, and pushed her cart down the aisle.

"You, too. Have a good day."

Sari took a few deep breaths and turned back to her work. She had started her shift excited about going out on a date with Damon the next evening, but after her conversation with his mother, she was second-guessing pretty much everything. She wasn't mad at Kimberly—the woman knew what it was like to be a single mom. The things she'd said really hadn't been out of line. It just sucked to hear them said aloud.

The rest of Sari's workday dragged. She was not having the good day she'd thought she'd have when she'd gotten out of bed.

The next morning, Sari was trying to do something about the puffy bags under her eyes. She had not slept well because Kimberly's warning had tumbled around in her head like marbles in a glass jar, causing a commotion and threatening to crack her well-ordered life. All of her original worries about dating a younger, carefree guy had resurfaced for her to reanalyze and fret over.

Tonight, they'd have some uninterrupted alone time to talk about all the things weighing on her mind. She just wasn't sure what all she wanted to say, but she had the day to think about it.

As the morning wore on, she got herself more wound up, and by the time work called to ask if she could take an afternoon into evening shift for someone who was sick, she didn't say no. She told herself it was because she needed to show them that she was serious about her job and moving into management, but it was really just her avoiding a tough conversation she didn't know how to have. She could use the extra money and time to think about what was best for her and her children in the long run.

Now she needed to tell Damon she had to cancel their date night. She hoped he hadn't gone to too much trouble.

Damon smiled when his new doorbell chimed with a normal sound that didn't make him wince. He'd just finished making the final plans for tonight's date and was really looking forward to the evening. Before he could even get the door all the way open, Benjy was pushing his way inside.

"Surprise visit," the little boy said, and then hugged his leg.

"'Prise," Jacob echoed his big brother and hugged his other leg.

Happy for the visit, he tousled the boys' hair. "What are you two squirts up to?"

"Nothin'. Just gonna play," Benjy said as they headed into the living room and the basket of toys.

"Boys," Sari called after them, "remember we can only stay for a few minutes."

"Okay, Mama."

Sari stepped inside the entryway. "Hi."

"Hello, beautiful." He wrapped his arms around her waist and stole a quick kiss.

"Sorry for just popping by, but you forgot this on my bedside table." She held up her wrist to show his watch that was much too big and slid down halfway to her elbow. "I thought you might need it. And it was a good excuse to see you."

"You don't need an excuse to come over. I need to check something in the oven. Come into the kitchen with me."

"A frozen pizza?"

"Maybe," he said with a chuckle. "Have y'all had lunch?"

"Yes. We already ate."

He adored this woman and her kids and was happy for the unexpected visit. Tonight, he was planning to tell her he was in love with her. And if everything went as planned and they were on the same page, they could discuss where they might go from here. He was starting to think about them eventually getting to the point where she could go back to school if she wanted to, or she could be a stay-at-home mom. Now that he had money, all kinds of ideas were taking root. He had the means to make things happen, and making life easier for Sari and the boys was something he really wanted to do. Something he wished someone had done for him when he was a kid.

"Am I still watching the boys tomorrow afternoon while you and Alana go for pedicures?"

"If you're still available."

"I am. Coop said he'd come over and hang out with us and we'll give the boys dinner."

"That works."

Sari seemed distracted, and he had an uncomfortable feeling something was bothering her. She leaned her hip against the kitchen counter and pulled at the collar of one of the white shirts she always wore under her purple GreatStore apron.

"Wait. Why are you dressed like you are going to work? Aren't you off all day today?"

Her sigh came from deep down. "I was, but they're shorthanded today because of several people out sick, and since I want to move into management, I have to stay on their good side. I need to show them I'm serious about my job. They did say I might not have to stay the whole shift if they can find someone to take over, but I'm afraid it would be too late to make tonight's date."

Damon's stomach was twisting, and all his plans felt like they were in jeopardy. Not the reservations and date stuff, but the life plans. The things he'd been planning to tell her. To say he was disappointed was an understatement. "You need a different job with more regular hours."

She rubbed her temples as if she had a headache. "Damon, I'm doing the best I can.

"Honey, I'm not implying that you aren't. You know how much I admire you and your strength. I just want you to be happy and taken care of."

"I have never asked you to take care of me. I don't need you to be my real-life superhero." She pushed away from the counter. "In fact, I've told you I do not need anyone taking care of me. We've talked about this. I can't let myself depend on anyone else."

"Sari—"

"From the beginning, I've tried to make you understand that my life is very busy and can be unpredictable. Benjy and Jacob are counting on me, and I warned you that I would not have time or energy for a relationship. My main focus must be on being the best mom I can be, because I'm all the boys have."

"They have me, too."

"But for how long? We only agreed to hang out with no expectations. No commitments."

His heart felt as if it had a vise clamping down on it, slowly squeezing the hope from his body. He'd thought they were past all the "no commitments" bull He wanted to be more to her and the boys than someone she "hung out with." But she was not in a state of mind to hear what he wanted to say.

"I need to get going or I'll be late for work. I'm sorry about canceling tonight. I hope you didn't go to too much trouble."

"It's fine." He had gone to quite a bit of trouble, but he wasn't going to admit that and make her feel worse or make himself look…desperate. And he might need to reconsider a few things he'd been planning to say. He drew her into a hug and kissed the top of her head. "I hope you have a good day at work."

She kissed him, then stepped away. "I'll see you tomorrow."

Which meant she wasn't even going to ask him to come over after she got off work.

After Sari and the boys left, he changed into shorts and went for a long run. He needed the physical exertion and the uninterrupted time to think. But he got nothing resolved.

How could he show her that he was responsible and would help make her life easier and not more complicated?

An hour later, drenched in sweat and out of breath, Damon closed his front door behind him, then abruptly stopped and cocked his head. There was music playing. Music that he had definitely not left on.

Chapter Twenty-Three

Every hair on Damon's body spiked up at once.

Someone was in his house. But would a burglar be playing a country music ballad while robbing him? He let out the breath he'd been holding, then on an inhale, he caught the savory scent of bacon wafting from the kitchen, and then distinctly female humming coming from his bedroom.

Relaxing even more, his grin widened as he toed off his running shoes and tucked them under the entryway bench. Sari must have gotten out of work and was here to surprise him. Her car wasn't in the driveway beside his, so she must have used the new garage door opener he'd given her. All he knew was that he was damn glad to come home and find her here.

Damon made his way to his bedroom, and instantly went from excited and turned on to...

"Katie?"

"Hi, Damon." She smiled as she came out of the en suite bathroom. "I hope you don't mind that I used the hidden key you showed me before I moved out of town. Since your car is here, I figured you'd gone for a run. I wanted to surprise you with a favorite meal."

"Oh, wow." He remembered telling her she could use the key anytime, but he had meant *while* they were dating. Not once she'd moved away and had no idea what was going on in his love life. "How did you get here?"

"I walked from my parents' house. I wanted to take you up on that rain check before I have to fly home. But now that I think about it, I should have called you rather than making it a surprise."

"At first, I thought you were a burglar."

She clasped her hands and pressed them against her chin. "I'm sorry. Bad judgment on my part."

"Well, I was surprised," he said with a chuckle. He didn't want her to know he was disappointed it was her and not Sari. "Let's go talk in the kitchen, because something smells delicious." He needed to get her out of his bedroom. And even though he really needed a shower, he did not want her to get any ideas about joining him.

In the kitchen he saw bacon-wrapped jalapeños, the makings for chili-cheese hot dogs and a giant cinnamon roll. Not a meal Sari would even consider serving to him. "This looks really good. Let's eat and talk."

They filled their plates and sat at opposite ends of his table.

"I should have been more honest with you when you asked me to go to Austin."

She wiped her mouth with a napkin and studied him. "You're dating someone." It wasn't a question, and she gave him a sad smile.

"Not exactly. It's…"

It's what? What am I doing with Sari?

He had not been out on a date with another woman since the night he met Sari. And having Katie here made him jumpy and nervous, like he was doing something he shouldn't. "It's complicated." Damon was surprised when her smile brightened.

"Oh. My. God. It's happened."

"What?"

"Damon the ladies' man has fallen in love and become a one-woman man."

"I—" He cut himself off from denying it. He *was* in love. But he didn't have to admit anything to Katie. "I've been dating one woman for a while now. I should have told you right away."

"It's okay. I'm just in town for a visit and you don't owe me explanations. I'm glad to see you happy."

But was he happy about this revelation? He stuffed half of a jalapeño popper into his mouth and let the heat of the pepper burn comfortably as he chewed. A one-sided love with Sari was not what was supposed to happen.

Once they'd finished eating and Katie made it clear that she really was happy for him, she left, wishing him well in his relationship with Sari. He closed the front door behind her and got straight into the shower. With wet hair and a clean pair of running shorts, he grabbed a beer and walked into his backyard, wishing he at least had a pet to break up the silence.

Damon had broken a few hearts in his day. Never on purpose, but it had happened. Was he about to discover what it felt like, firsthand?

The next afternoon, Damon was in the backyard opening the clubhouse when Sari and the boys came around the side of the house. Benjy and Jacob ran to him for hugs before going off to play.

Without a word, Sari wrapped her arms around his neck and swayed for a moment in his embrace. "I'm sorry about yesterday."

He stroked her hair from the crown of her head and down along the length of her back, the knot in his gut twisting. "We can always schedule another date. No worries."

"I mean…" She lifted her head and held his gaze. "I'm sorry about the way I acted and the things I said."

"Did something happen that upset you?" he asked.

She shook her head like she was wishing something away, and he got the feeling there was something she wasn't saying. "I just started getting in my head and overthinking things."

"Are y'all going to stay here tonight after you and Alana get back? I'd love a chance to talk."

"Yes. We brought our things. What do you want to talk about?"

"Life."

She grinned. "Pretty broad topic. That might take longer than a night."

And that was exactly what he wanted. But he wasn't going to say that. Not until they had an uninterrupted block of time.

Before they got any deeper into the topic, Coop and Alana arrived and the ladies got ready to go to their pedicure appointments and dinner out.

"I need kisses from my boys," Sari said, then knelt in the grass before them. "I love you, my sweeties."

Benjy kissed her cheek. "Love you, Mama."

"Bye, bye," Jacob said in his cute baby voice, and puckered for a kiss.

"Listen to Damon and Mr. Cooper and do what they say."

"Okay." Benjy ran for the clubhouse.

Damon held out a hand to help her up. "Do you need a kiss from me, too?"

"I think I do." She raised onto her toes and glanced

over his shoulder to where the kids played with Coop and Alana. "Keep it PG. For now."

"We'll call it a preview of later tonight." He pressed his mouth lightly to hers, barely teasing her lips with the tip of his tongue. Her soft moan wrapped around him every bit as much as her arms.

This woman felt so right against him. For the first time in ages, he was dating a woman, with no desire to ask out any others, but he couldn't tell her that. She was too skittish.

"I should get going."

"Have fun. Your boys will be just fine."

"They better be." She grinned at him and then motioned for Alana to join her, and they headed around the side of the house toward the car.

Damon joined his brother and the kids by the sandbox. "Did Alana think you needed babysitting practice? Is that why you're here?"

"Are you kidding? I came for ice cream night."

"Did you get the bananas? Sari likes them to have some fruit with every meal."

"I got the bananas. Do the cherries in a jar count as fruit?"

"Probably not." He watched Benjy scoop a handful of sand and hold it above his little brother's head. "Benjy, don't do it."

The little boy moved his hand in front of him and let the sand trickle through his fingers back into the sandbox. "Do what? I wasn't going to do anything."

Coop laughed. "That kid reminds me of you at that age."

"Oh, yeah? I must have been pretty cool. What else did you get at the grocery store?"

"Three flavors of ice cream, four different kinds of sundae sauce and tons of other toppings. And a can of whipped cream."

Damon was starting to feel a twinge of worry that he should have asked Sari about giving the boys ice cream. But she let them have special treats on occasion, and what better time than boys' night?

They played outside with the kids until everyone got too hot and then watched the cartoon version of a superhero movie. After that, Damon and Cooper set up the ice cream buffet on the patio picnic table. That would make it easy to hose off the mess that was sure to happen.

"Is anyone hungry?" Damon called to the boys as he neared the clubhouse.

"I am," Benjy yelled.

"We're having something special for dinner tonight."

"Cookies?" the four-year-old asked with a hopeful grin.

"Even better. Come see." He picked up Jacob and they made their way across the yard to the patio.

Jacob clasped his tiny hands to his cheeks. "Ice cweam."

"We get to eat all this?" Benjy asked and spread his arms wide.

Coop chuckled. "Not all of it, but I'm sure you'll get plenty."

He cocked his head at Damon. "I get to eat ice cream for dinner?"

"It's what happens on boys' night. We used to have ice cream night once a month when we were younger." *I really hope your mother will understand.*

"And then we would watch an action movie," Coop said.

"I think the boys are a little young for that part, unless you consider *PAW Patrol* an action cartoon."

Cooper demonstrated how to make a banana split and then told them about the options. Damon made a smaller one for Jacob and then seated him on his lap while his brother helped Benjy. By the time they got going, he realized the table and patio weren't the only things that would need to be hosed down. Cooper was the only one who had managed to remain relatively clean. Damon even had ice cream in his hair from Jacob waving his spoon around.

They were sticky and laughing and having a great time. Didn't every kid need someone who would spoil them now and then?

Sari and Alana sat in a faux cowhide-covered booth in the Saddle & Spur Roadhouse. While Alana enjoyed a cheeseburger and fries, that Sari wished she had ordered, she picked at her chicken tender salad. She was more interested in the two women who were trying to sneak looks at her, but they weren't very good at being covert.

"What are you staring at so hard?" Alana asked as she swirled a fry in ketchup.

"The redhead and the brunette at the table in the back corner. I'm trying to read their lips."

Her friend arched one eyebrow. "Why?"

"I think they're talking about us. Do you know them?"

Alana casually glanced at the two young women. "I don't know them, but they probably are talking about us. And I can make a pretty good guess what they might be saying."

"What?" Sari's knee was bouncing rapidly under the table.

"Damon is wealthy now. You've taken the most in-demand bachelor off the market. The last of the single Fortune Maloneys."

"I haven't 'taken' him," Sari said in a whispered yell. "It's not like we're even in a serious relationship."

Alana coughed around a choked laugh. "Is that what you tell yourself?"

With a groan, Sari propped her elbows on the table and covered her face with her hands. "You're right. Several times now, people have mistaken the four of us for a family."

"I'm not surprised."

"We were only supposed to hang out and have fun for a while. It was never supposed to become a serious relationship." Sari sighed. "But we have drifted into one anyway."

"Is that so bad? Damon really likes you."

"But for how long? Now that he has his money, he's going to start traveling. It probably won't be long until…" She swirled her hand in the air as if grasping for the right words. "Until he moves on."

"Talk to him and see how he's feeling about things."

"I have to think about my boys, and they're getting attached to Damon. I need to talk to them and prepare them for when he's not around anymore."

Alana put a hand on Sari's arm, the large diamond in her engagement ring catching the light and glistening. "That's why you don't want a relationship? Because of the kids?"

"Damon is young and carefree. At some point he'll get tired of dating a single mom with lots of responsibilities. I can't just take off on weekend trips or exotic vacations. Besides, I know his reputation for dating a lot of different women."

"I haven't seen or heard of him dating anyone else since he met you. And it is not for a lack of women trying to get a date with him."

Sari clasped her hands over her ears like one of her children might. "Don't even tell me about them."

"Want my advice?" Alana asked, and pushed her empty plate aside.

"Sure."

"Don't worry about what other people think or say. Believe me, I know what it's like to be the topic of gossip. Because I used to be a big flirt and dated a lot, people talked. It did bother me at first, but I know the truth of what's in my heart and the way people can be. I've grown used to people talking about me, and I've learned to blow it off."

Sari let out a long sigh. "You're right. I shouldn't let it bother me, but I should have a serious conversation with Damon sooner rather than later. But enough about that for now. Tell me something else good going on in your life."

"We made an offer on the ranch I was telling you about."

"That's wonderful. Benjy keeps talking about riding a horse with cowboy Coop."

"That's so cute. That can definitely be arranged. Are you ready to go?" Alana put cash on top of the bill that she insisted on paying.

"Yes. Thank you again for treating me to dinner out."

As they were walking out the front door, they just happened to be behind the two women who had been looking at her.

"You know why she's dating Damon, right?" asked the redhead.

"For the sex?" the other said.

"No. Well...maybe that, too, but I bet it's for the Fortune money."

Sari's jaw tensed, but she decided not to be angry. "It's for the sex," she said, and almost laughed at the startled looks on the women's faces when they turned and saw she was behind them.

"Sorry," both of them mumbled, and then hurried away with red faces.

"That'll teach them," Alana said, working hard to control her own laughter.

Of course having money was nice. Sari saw the difference it had made in Alana's life. But more than most people, she knew it wasn't everything.

When they got back to Damon's house, Sari left Alana inside talking on the phone and went into the backyard. What she found made her chin drop enough that her jaw made a cracking sound. The four of them were sitting at the table that was covered with drips of ice cream, smears of chocolate sauce and dollops of oozing whipped cream, along with melted-together stuff she couldn't even identify. Benjy and Jacob's faces were covered with ice cream. Jacob even had some in his hair.

"What in the world is going on here? What happened to eating a healthy dinner?"

"Mama, ice cream splits. It has banana and that's a fruit," Benjy hurried to add.

"Ice cweam," Jacob echoed his big brother from his seat on Damon's lap.

"I can see that." She was working hard to control her expression so she wouldn't upset her children—who were not to blame for this unapproved ice cream fiasco.

Damon glanced at the sticky child on his lap, then met her gaze with a contrite expression that made him look like one of the kids. "I'm sorry."

Jacob waved his spoon and ice cream splatted on Damon's forehead.

Cooper, who had been frozen in place, bolted inside the house but didn't get far before bursting into laughter.

Damon held perfectly still while the glob of chocolate slid down his face and landed on his shirt. "I deserved that." He licked the ice cream from the corner of his mouth and grabbed a paper towel.

"Something we can agree on," she said through clenched teeth. Even though she was angry, she had to control her own urge to laugh at the sight of Damon.

Benjy kept shoveling his treat into his mouth as if knowing it was about to be taken away.

Cooper stepped back out onto the patio and cleared his throat. "It's mostly my fault. It was my idea to resurrect ice cream night like we used to do when we were kids."

"I appreciate you telling me," she said. "Let's get you boys washed up so we can go home."

"But, Mama, you said we can stay here tonight," Benjy said, then immediately shoved another bite into his mouth.

"Sorry, boys. Not tonight." She was in no state of mind to have a serious conversation with Damon after coming back to find this huge mess.

Damon put Jacob on his feet and stood. "Coop, will you take them over to that water hose and help them get cleaned up?"

"Sure. Come on, you two, let's go over here."

"I was wrong to let this happen," Damon said.

"Damon, you don't get what it means to be a full-time parent. It's easy for you to be Mr. Fun Guy. I don't have the luxury of being the 'good cop.' If I mess up, they suffer."

"Sari, honey." He came forward but she held up a hand palm out.

"I need a minute." What she really needed was a rewind button so she could go back and… What? What would she do if she got a do-over?

Chapter Twenty-Four

Damon's stomach roiled and he regretted eating so much ice cream, but more than that, he regretted upsetting Sari. The disappointed expression on her face was gutting him.

"I told you why I do what I do. I told you about their dad," she said almost in a whisper.

"What can I do to make this right?"

Jacob ran up to him and held up his arms. "Daddy, up."

Sari gasped and covered her mouth with her hand.

Damon could hear his blood rushing in his head, but not wanting to hurt Jacob's feelings, he picked up the wet, smiling child and patted his little back. He watched the expression on Sari's face go from shock to something he didn't want to put a name to.

The seconds ticked by, every one of them building with tension that hung heavy in the air. Her silence was killing him.

Jacob touched his cheek, the sweet child unaware
of the storm brewing. He tried to smile back at him,
but the hot prickly knot in his throat made it difficult.

Sari made a choked sound, and he steeled himself
for what he feared was coming next.

"What have I done?" she whispered, her voice
trembling with emotion. "I'm sorry. This has to be
over. It's time."

No! What is she saying? She can't mean it.

"Sari, honey—"

"We knew from the very beginning that this time
would come." She held out her arms for her son,
making an obvious effort not to touch Damon in
the process. "Benjy, please come with me to the car,
now."

Benjy started to argue but snapped his little mouth
shut, no doubt reading the expression on his mother's
face. He hugged Damon's leg.

He knelt to the little boy's eye level. "Be good,
kid."

"Okay. See you later," he said, and then followed
his mother.

Will I see him later? Did I just ruin everything?

There was more to this than just the ice cream.
Something had been building over the last few days.

Jacob waved over her shoulder, but Sari did not

look back at him. Not even a quick glance. They disappeared into the house, and Damon ran his hands roughly through his hair, mumbling a few choice cuss words.

"Did you just break up?" his brother asked.

"I think so."

"Bro, I'm sorry. I shouldn't have brought all this ice cream." He nodded toward the melting mess on the picnic table.

"It's not your fault. I could have stopped you. I *should* have said no. It was my responsibility to look out for them." He leaned his back against the brick wall beside the sliding glass door, his legs suddenly feeling too weak to hold him. "She's right. I'm not ready to be a parent. This was never part of the plan."

"I don't think anyone is ever ready to be a parent." Cooper started cleaning up the mess.

"You seem ready."

His brother barked a quick laugh. "I'm excited for Alana to have the baby, but ready is a different matter entirely. Maybe Sari just needs some time to cool off."

Time. He shivered. She'd just told him that their time had run out. "I think I know a big part of the problem. She doesn't want me to take the place of her husband in her heart or her kids' hearts."

He knew what was happening to his own heart. It was on the verge of shattering, and it hurt more than he ever could have imagined.

* * *

Sari's hands were still trembling when she got home and unlocked her front door. Jacob calling him daddy had totally freaked her out.

How could I let this happen?

She'd let Damon get too close and let her boys get too attached to him. Her precious little boys were going to be hurt by this breakup, and it was all her fault. Her heart was not going to go unscathed, either. It was already breaking.

She dropped onto her red chair just as Benjy walked up and stood in front of her.

"Mama, are you mad at me?" Benjy asked, his lip quivering.

"Oh, sweetheart, no." She pulled him onto her lap and hugged him tight, kissing the top of his head and his cheeks. "I'm not mad at you at all. You didn't do anything wrong."

"Are you mad at Damon?"

She took a long slow breath and stroked his hair. She didn't want to lie to her son. "Yes, I am."

"Why?"

"Because he knew you were supposed to eat healthy food before having dessert."

"Oh." He slid off her lap. "I'll tell him to say sorry and give you a hug and kiss and make it all better."

She held her breath to hold back a sob that would scare her son. If only hugs and kisses could make it better. "Go pick out the pajamas you want to wear, and we'll have a bath. I love you," she called after him.

"Love you, too, Mama."

Sari leaned forward and dropped her head into her hands.

She knew Damon cared for her, but he had never expressed love. And they had never discussed a future together. But that sure hadn't stopped her from being a big fool and falling in love. For all of their sakes, she needed to end things. There was no reason to wait around for her boys to get even more attached and for Damon to grow tired of all the responsibilities of being with her.

She struggled to put on a cheery face during bath and story time, but once she tucked them in and turned off the lights, it was a different story. She cried in the shower. She cried in bed. And she might have even cried in her sleep.

The drone of the living room TV echoed around Damon, but he wasn't paying the least bit of attention. He was too focused on the bottle of beer in his hand and the ache that had taken up residence in the center of this chest. Thank God he'd quit his job after getting his money, because he was in no condition to smile and chat with customers. He'd even scared away two of his brothers when they'd stopped by to check on him.

She hadn't responded to his calls or text messages,

and he had stopped trying. He should have known from day one with Sari that only "hanging out" would be impossible.

He tipped back the bottle for a long pull that finished it off. When he thunked the empty bottle on the coffee table, a bag of chips spilled its contents down the other side. It was probably time to do something about the mess, but he didn't care that the coffee table was covered with three days' worth of take-out containers and various empty bottles, cans and Styrofoam cups.

How many more days am I going to let myself be pathetic?

His mother would have a fit if she saw this disaster, and he should clean it up before she stopped by—even though he'd told her he was fine and just wanted a few days to be alone. If she saw the empty bottles, she'd tell him that anyone who drank alone was on the road to ruin. He stood, looked at the trash and then sat back down. One more day wouldn't hurt anything.

Damon inhaled deeply, then winced. "Oh man, I need a shower. That can't wait." He turned off the TV and headed to the bathroom.

After a hot shower, he wiped the moisture from the mirror and sneered at himself. "This is what you said you wanted all along, dumbass."

He was single, loaded, and free to party and date whoever and however many women he wanted.

There was one problem, though. He didn't want to go on a date with another woman or kiss another woman. Hell, he didn't even want to call one, because he no longer had the heart for casual dating. His beautiful, flame-haired Sari was the only one he wanted.

This was what it felt like to give your heart away. And here was problem number two. Sari wasn't *his* anything. Never had been, for that matter. He'd just chosen to ignore that bit of information. He'd fallen in love with Sari, and he loved the boys, but they weren't his to love. She was clearly not going to let him take Seth's place.

He finally knew what he wanted in life…but he just couldn't have it.

"Fool. I'm as dumb as my brothers always tell me I am." In nothing but a towel around his waist, he left the bathroom and flopped facedown onto his bed. He'd figure out what to do with himself tomorrow.

Chapter Twenty-Five

Sari had clocked out from her shift, shopped for groceries and picked up the boys from day care, and they were almost home.

"Mama, are we going to Damon's house?" Benjy asked as he swung his feet in rhythm with the song, gently kicking the back of her seat.

"Day-me's house?" Jacob asked.

It gutted her every time they asked for him and she had no choice but to deny them. How was Damon dealing with their breakup? He'd left a few messages saying they should talk, but she didn't know what to say. She hadn't seen him anywhere around town over the last few days and had not had the heart to ask anyone.

"I'm sorry, boys. Remember we talked about this. He is very busy and probably not even in town."

"But we miss him, Mama."

"I know he misses you, too." Her throat burned as she swallowed back tears, which she'd also had to do several times during her shift at GreatStore today. She missed him like crazy but letting Benjy and Jacob, or herself, get any closer to him was a terribly risky idea. A chance she couldn't take. "Do you want to stop at the park for a few minutes before we go home?"

"No," Benjy sighed. "Our clubhouse at Damon's is funner."

Of course it is.

The problem was, she couldn't disagree. Damon had created a magical place for children in his big backyard. The question that kept tickling the back of her mind was, why had he done it?

Her skin tingled. Could it be because…

No. I can't keep wishing things were different.

She hated seeing her boys so sad, but she was doing it for them. Protecting them was her job. She was glad that she'd put a box of the mini-sized ice cream treats into her shopping cart. Was she bribing her sons with the exact thing she'd gotten so mad at Damon about? Sadly, yes. But they were all hurting and needed a way to get through the adjustment of being just the three of them again.

After a dinner of grilled chicken, Sari pulled two mini ice cream sandwiches from the freezer. "Boys,

I have a special treat for dessert." She wiggled them in the air.

"Yay!" Benjy yelled, and Jacob clapped his hands.

She handed one to Benjy and went around the table to unwrap the other one for Jacob.

"You have one, too, Mama."

"I think I will." She grabbed one for herself.

The giggles and smiles were worth the mess that required a trip directly to the bathtub. She even got a sticky kiss on her cheek from a happy little boy. Getting them to bed a little early sounded like a great idea. She was exhausted from work and the stress of being sad about Damon and could use some time alone to...

To do what? What am I going to do? Cry? Mope around missing a man who I knew would never be mine?

Sari started the boys' bathwater and helped Jacob get undressed. She bathed them and then sat on the lid of the toilet while they splashed and played with their toy boats.

She'd known from the beginning that hanging out with Damon wasn't a forever kind of thing. She told him as much multiple times. What did a young, good-looking single guy—who was now a million-aire—want long-term with a widow and two toddlers? He'd just wanted to hang out with her and play the "fun uncle" to some cute kids for a little while.

This didn't stop her from missing having Damon

around to make her laugh and to hold her at night. Several times a day she considered calling him to apologize for the abrupt way she'd ended things, but a clean break was best.

This whole wonderful, painful experience had taught her something important. Now she knew she was capable of loving again. It was just unfortunate she had to discover this by falling in love with Damon.

Sari woke in the night to the sound of a child crying.

"Mama."

She sat up in bed. It was Jacob. She rushed across the hallway to their room. "What's the matter, sweet boy?"

He whimpered and wrapped his little arms around her, and her adrenaline spiked. He was burning up with fever. With her two-year-old cradled against her, she carried him to the bathroom and got the digital thermometer out of the medicine cabinet. She held it to Jacob's forehead and gasped when the screen turned red and displayed a fever of 103 degrees.

"Oh, no. Mama is going to make it better, sweetie."

Right away, she gave him a dose of liquid fever reducer and put a cold wet washcloth around his neck, but this made him shiver and cry harder. Jacob had spiked a high fever in the past, and she knew she needed to get him to the emergency room. But it was the middle of the night, and she needed help with Benjy. Her first thought was to call Mrs. Mata, but then Sari remembered that she was out of town to visit family.

She laid Jacob on her bed and quickly pulled on a pair of jeans and the shirt she'd worn yesterday. She rushed across the hall to the boys' room and gently shook Benjy. "Sweetheart, I need you to wake up. We need to get in the car and take Jacob to the doctor."

He mumbled and tried to roll over and go back to sleep. She needed help, but there weren't many people she could call at this hour.

"Damon," she whispered to herself. She couldn't think of anyone else, and he cared for the boys. Surely he would come to help them.

She grabbed her phone from her bedside table and dialed his number. He picked up on the second ring.

"Sari, what's wrong?"

"It's Jacob. He's sick with a 103 fever. I need to take him to the emergency room." She paused to catch her breath before she started hyperventilating. "I need help with Benjy." She heard rustling and then a door slammed on his end of the call.

"I'm headed to my car now," he said.

"Will you meet me at the emergency room?"

"I'll be there."

She hung up and lifted Benjy into a sitting position. "I need you to wake up. Do you want to see Damon?"

That got him to open his eyes. "Damon?"

"Yes, but we need to get in the car as fast as we can. Can you get your shoes and move like Mr. Lightning?"

He scrambled out of bed and pulled his shoes on. She picked up Jacob and grabbed her purse, and they hurried to the car.

On the drive, Benjy was patting his brother's arm and telling him it would be okay because Damon was coming. She wasn't sure how to feel about that.

She parked in a spot near the ER door and first got Benjy out and then Jacob, who was no longer crying but was whimpering in a way that sent her pulse racing. With Benjy keeping pace beside her she rushed through the sliding doors and up to the reception counter.

"Can I help you?" said a man with gray hair and thick glasses.

"Yes, my son has a 103 fever."

The sliding doors whooshed open behind her, and Damon rushed in. Benjy ran to him, and he picked up the child. "Hey, kiddo."

Sari felt some of her tension ease. "Thanks for coming."

"I've got him, honey." He came close enough to kiss Jacob's forehead. "Go do what you need to."

At the nurse's direction, she carried Jacob back to an exam room. Thank goodness for Damon.

Damon put Benjy on his feet and watched Sari carry Jacob out of sight. His heart rate settled into a somewhat normal rhythm for the first time since getting Sari's frantic call.

"Jacob is sick," Benjy said. "Will they make him all better?"

"Yes, they will." *Please God, let that be true.* "Let's find a place to sit down." He took the little boy's hand, and they went over to a seating area with a blue couch.

Benjy yawned. "Mama woke me up. I hurried like lightning because she said I got to see you."

The ache that had decided to take up residence in his chest gave an extra squeeze. "I sure am glad to see you. I've missed you, too." He hugged him and the little boy yawned. "Why don't you rest your head on my lap and go back to sleep." Benjy did as he'd asked, and he stroked his red hair.

Damon took a long, slow breath. When his phone had rung with Sari's number, he'd answered without a second thought, because he'd known something was wrong for her to call him at one in the morning. He had been awake, sitting in front of the TV and missing Sari and the boys like crazy.

Benjy fell asleep a few minutes later and then Sari came into the waiting area. She looked tired and frazzled and beautiful. He would have jumped to his feet if he hadn't had a sleeping child on his lap. "Is Jacob okay?"

"Yes, he'll be okay." She sat beside her son's feet.

"I can't stay out here long but I wanted to say thank you for coming so quickly."

"Of course. I'm glad you called me. What's wrong with him? Does he need to stay overnight?"

"No. We'll be going home after another couple of hours. They're just waiting for a few test results and they're giving him antibiotics and fluids."

He wanted so badly to hold her and comfort her, but the way they'd left things... He didn't know what was okay to do. "Do you want me to stay here with you or take Benjy home?"

"You should take him back to my apartment. But you'll need his booster seat."

"I'll swap it over to my car. I'm parked right beside you."

She stayed with Benjy in the waiting area long enough for him to rush outside and transfer the booster seat to his 4Runner. She gave him her house key, and when she leaned in to kiss Damon's cheek, her scent wrapped around him, making him miss her more than ever.

When they got to her apartment, the little boy didn't want to go to his bed because he wanted to stay up with Damon. He let him fall asleep beside him once again while they watched TV and then carried him to his bed.

When Sari came through the door a little over an

hour later with a sleeping child cradled against her shoulder, he got up. "How is he?"

"Much better," she whispered.

"Good. Should I go?" *Please ask me to stay.*

"If you'll wait for me to go put him in my bed, I'd like to talk to you."

"I'll be right here."

She was back within a couple of minutes, and she sat in her red chair. "Damon, I'm sorry."

He wasn't sure if she was apologizing for calling him in the middle of the night or something else. "I was happy to come help. Anytime."

"Not that. Well…that, too. But I'm sorry about pushing you away." A tear rolled down her cheek.

"Sweetheart, come here." He stood and opened his arms and she eased into his embrace.

"I pushed you away and said things I regret." She held him a little tighter and rested her head against him. "I've missed you."

"I've missed you, too. So much."

Sari yawned. "I'm so tired."

He didn't want to let go of her, but he knew she needed her rest. "You should get some sleep."

She raised her head from his chest. "Will you stay? We can talk more in the morning and the boys will want to see you."

"Of course. I can sleep on the couch."

"That would be great."

His heart started beating at what felt like a normal rhythm for the first time since they'd ended things. "I'd like that."

But he couldn't let himself jump to the conclusion that everything was right between them again.

Chapter Twenty-Six

Sari woke with the sun, the memory of last night's emergency bringing her immediately into full consciousness. Jacob was sleeping peacefully beside her. She kissed his forehead, glad to discover he was no longer burning with fever. She got out of bed and went to look in on Benjy, but he wasn't in his room. In the living room, Damon was sound asleep on the couch with Benjy beside him. Their features and coloring were nothing alike, but they were both sleeping with an arm above their head, and they were both beautiful. And she loved them.

She stroked her fingers across Damon's cheek and his eyes fluttered open. "Good morning," she whispered.

He clasped her hand and kissed her palm. "Good

morning, beautiful." He then focused on Benjy, brushing his hair back from his forehead. "How is Jacob?"

"He's better." Looking at the two of them now, it reminded her of last night when she'd come out of the exam room and seen him stroking Benjy's head while he slept. Even in the middle of an emergency, it had been a beautiful sight that she'd always remember. It made her want something more for herself and her children. It made her want the kind of family life she and Seth had dreamed about, and she knew it was something he would want for his sons and for her.

But could she have that with Damon?

"I'm going to go make some coffee and leave Jacob to sleep."

"I'll meet you in the kitchen in a few minutes."

Sari was standing in front of the coffee maker watching it drip when he came up behind her and wrapped his arms around her waist to kiss the side of her neck. She realized that she could count on Damon, and that he could be serious when needed.

"Damon, I'm really glad you're here."

"Me, too. I've been completely miserable without you and the boys."

Sari turned in his arms so she could see his eyes. "The boys asked for you every day." She kissed him softly. "And so did my heart."

He flashed his crooked grin. "You don't know how happy that makes me. If I can be a part of your lives again, I promise never to give them ice cream without checking with you."

She recalled Benjy's face as he'd shoveled in spoonfuls of ice cream as fast as he could, fearing she was going to snatch it away from him. Was Damon right? Was she being over-the-top with her food rules?

She pressed a hand to her mouth and her eyes got wide. "Oh my God. What am I doing? I'm making us all crazy with my strict food rules." She stepped away from him to pace across her small kitchen. "It doesn't matter if I eat freaking pizza and ice cream all day or boring salad and tofu. I could still drop dead at any second and leave my boys just like their father did. Seth was very healthy, but he died anyway."

He caught hold of her hand as she went by. "You have more people in your life now. If the worst were to happen, Benjy and Jacob would be loved."

She pressed her fingertips to her forehead. "How can you be sure of that?"

Gently cradling her face, he waited until she looked at him. "Because I love them. Your children have found their way into my heart, and I would never let anything happen to either of them. Or to you."

"You would really raise my boys if something happened to me?"

"Yes, I would. But nothing is going to happen to

you." When she made a sound of disagreement, he brushed the corner of her mouth with his thumb. "And before you say it, I know there's no guarantee, but what happened to Seth was a shocking tragedy. A rare one for someone his age."

"That's true."

"I don't want to take Seth's place in your heart or theirs. Let me love you. Let me love the boys."

She smiled as some of her tension released. "It has only taken me a few days away from you to realize I need you in my life. What's more... I want you in our lives. I love you, Damon."

His smile was tender, and his eyes were filled with emotion. "I have loved you from the moment I saw you. You've taught me the meaning of true love and commitment, and you're teaching me what it means to be a parent. You've made me a better man."

"What about your plans to go on big adventures?"

"A life with you three is all the adventure I need. When the boys are older, we can have adventures together."

There was a lightness in her chest that she couldn't remember feeling. "Are you really ready to make a commitment? A real, true forever commitment? You have to be in it not just for the long haul but for the forever haul."

"I look forward to forever with you, honey. I have never been so sure of anything. I love all three of you and I can't imagine my life without you. I know you don't need a real-life superhero, but I want to take care of you and the boys...forever."

If a heart could sing, hers would be performing a concert. "I think we make a pretty good team."

"The best." Cupping her cheek, he kissed her. A soft achingly sweet kiss that began to heal some of the hurt.

A child's giggle made them turn to the living room. "Are we a superhero team?" Benjy asked, and ran over to them.

Damon swooped him up into the air, eliciting more giggles. "You bet we are, squirt."

"Let's go get Jacob and tell him," Benjy said.

Minutes later, the four of them were cuddled together on her bed, Jacob thankfully feeling much better.

"I been thinkin'," Benjy said. "If we are a superhero team, what's our name?"

Damon held up a finger to signal he had an idea. "How about Team Fortune? Because I feel like the real fortune that I've gained has nothing to do with money. It's the three of you."

Sari did her best to gather all three of them into her arms at once, and with tears trickling down her cheeks, she kissed them. "I love my three boys so much."

Epilogue

Sari and the boys were officially moved out of the apartment and settled into their home with Damon. She had quit her job and enrolled in college to finish her degree. On a sunny afternoon, she and Damon were cuddled on the two-person hammock in his backyard while the boys played.

He laced his fingers with hers and kissed her knuckles. "Benjy and Jacob might not be my blood, but I've come to think of them as my boys. And I know I've missed a lot of firsts. First steps. First words. First tooth and so many others. But I want to be there for the rest of them. The first day of school and ball games and all the good as well as the bad."

"I think that's a wonderful idea."

He cleared his throat. "I have something very important to ask you."

"This sounds serious."

"It is. A good kind of serious." He shifted so he could see her face. "So, this might take some of the surprise out of my plans, but I'd like your permission to talk to the boys about becoming an official family."

Her smile wobbled with happy tears. "Hey, boys. Come over here for a minute," she called to them. "We need to talk to you."

Damon got out of the hammock and sat on the grass beside them, and Jacob immediately climbed into his lap. Benjy rolled onto his back and looked at Damon upside down.

"How do you two feel about us becoming a family? Both of you, your mom and me?"

"A family?" Benjy sprang up to his knees. "You would be like a daddy since mine is in heaven?"

Damon looked at Sari, and she nodded with a smile. He wanted them to have what he had not. Two parents to love and take care of them. He would never become a "leaver" like his own father and grandfather. It was time to break that cycle of pain. "Yes, that's right. I will take care of both of you and love you just like a daddy."

"Daddy," Jacob said, and patted Damon's shoulder.

"Yay!" Benjy tackled him and all three of them fell back onto the grass in a fit of giggles and hugs.

Sari couldn't resist and joined in on the cuddles. Their new gray kitten, Silver, came bounding over to join the family. The little bell on his bright purple collar jingling as he pounced onto Benjy.

"I have more to talk to you about. Something very important," Damon said to the boys. "Do I have your permission to marry your mama?"

"Yep," Benjy said. "I give you 'mission to marry Mama."

Damon's heart swelled with love for all three of them. "You boys will have cousins. My sister Justine has a little boy about Jacob's age. Remember my brother Coop who brought the ice cream?"

"And Mama got mad," Benjy said.

Damon grimaced as he looked at Sari, but she laughed. "Very soon, Coop is going to have a new baby, and then you will have two cousins to love."

Benjy looked concerned. "But if you love them, can you still love us, too? Will you still love me and Jacob best?"

He hugged both of them to his chest. "I have plenty of love to go around. Loving them will not take away any of my love for you."

"Okay. We can all love them," Benjy said, and picked up the kitten. "Let's go play, Jacob."

Once Damon untangled himself from the kids and made it to his feet, the boys ran back to their clubhouse.

"Stand up, honey." When she did, he dropped to

a knee before her and took one of her hands, making her suck in a sharp breath. "My sweet Sari, I love you more now than I did yesterday. More than five minutes ago, and I want to keep loving you forever. Will you marry me and make my world complete?"

"Yes, Damon. I will marry you and love you, forever." Sari was bursting with happiness, and when he stood, she threw herself into his arms and kissed him. "I also have an important question for you. Do you think you might have room in your heart for one more?"

His head cocked to the side. "One more?"

"I need to make another superhero cape. A tiny one." She put her hands against her stomach. "I'm having your baby."

His confusion shifted and a giant smile spread across his face as he lifted her off her feet with a spinning hug. "That's the most amazing news. I am so happy." Once he put her down, he kissed her cheeks and lips and then dropped to his knees to kiss her stomach, looking up at her with so much love.

"Thank you for making me the most fortunate man alive."

* * * * *

Look for the next installment of the new continuity
The Fortunes of Texas: Hitting the Jackpot
Don't miss

Self-Made Fortune
by USA TODAY *bestselling author Judy Duarte*
On sale May 2023, wherever Harlequin books
and ebooks are sold.

Catch up with the previous titles in
The Fortunes of Texas: Hitting the Jackpot
continuity

A Fortune's Windfall
by USA TODAY *bestselling author Michelle Major*

Fortune's Dream House
by Nina Crespo

Winning Her Fortune
by Heatherly Bell

Available now!

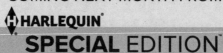

#2977 SELF-MADE FORTUNE

The Fortunes of Texas: Hitting the Jackpot • by Judy Duarte

Heiress Gigi Fortune has the hots for her handsome new lawyer! Harrison Vasquez may come from humble beginnings, but they have so much fun—in and out of bed! If only she can convince him their opposite backgrounds are the perfect ingredients for a shared future...

#2978 THE MARINE'S SECOND CHANCE

The Camdens of Montana • by Victoria Pade

The worst wound Major Dalton Camden ever received was the day Marli Abbott broke his heart. Now the fate of Marli's brother is in his hands...and Marli's back in town, stirring up all their old emotions. This time, they'll have to revisit the good *and* the bad to make their second-chance reunion permanent.

#2979 LIGHTNING STRIKES TWICE

Hatchet Lake • by Elizabeth Hrib

Newly single Kate Cardiff is in town to care for her sick father and his ailing ranch. The only problem? Annoying—and annoyingly sexy—ranch hand Nathan Prescott. Nathan will use every tool at his disposal to win over love-shy Kate. Starting with his knee-weakening kisses...

#2980 THE TROUBLE WITH EXES

The Navarros • by Sera Taíno

Dr. Nati Navarro's lucrative grant request is under review—by none other than her ex Leo Espinoza. But Leo is less interested in holding a grudge and much more interested in exploring their still-sizzling connection. Can Nati's lifelong dream include a career *and* romance this time around?

#2981 A CHARMING SINGLE DAD

Charming, Texas • by Heatherly Bell

How dare Rafe Reyes marry someone else! Jordan Del Toro knows she should let bygones be bygones. But when a wedding brings her face-to-face with her now-divorced ex—and his precious little girl—Jordan must decide if she wants revenge... or a new beginning with her old flame.

#2982 STARTING OVER AT TREVINO RANCH

Peach Leaf, Texas • by Amy Woods

Gina Heron wants to find a safe refuge in her small Texas hometown—*not* in Alex Trevino's strong arms. But reuniting with the boy she left behind is more powerful and exhilarating than a mustang stampede. The fiery-hot chemistry is still there. But can she prove she's no longer the cut-and-run type?

Get 4 FREE REWARDS!

We'll send you 2 FREE Books plus 2 FREE Mystery Gifts.

FREE
Value Over
$20

Both the **Harlequin® Special Edition** and **Harlequin® Heartwarming™** series feature compelling novels filled with stories of love and strength where the bonds of friendship, family and community unite.

YES! Please send me 2 FREE novels from the Harlequin Special Edition or Harlequin Heartwarming series and my 2 FREE gifts (gifts are worth about $10 retail). After receiving them, if I don't wish to receive any more books, I can return the shipping statement marked "cancel." If I don't cancel, I will receive 6 brand-new Harlequin Special Edition books every month and be billed just $5.49 each in the U.S. or $6.24 each in Canada, a savings of at least 12% off the cover price, or 4 brand-new Harlequin Heartwarming Larger-Print books every month and be billed just $6.24 each in the U.S. or $6.74 each in Canada, a savings of at least 19% off the cover price. It's quite a bargain! Shipping and handling is just 50¢ per book in the U.S. and $1.25 per book in Canada.* I understand that accepting the 2 free books and gifts places me under no obligation to buy anything. I can always return a shipment and cancel at any time by calling the number below. The free books and gifts are mine to keep no matter what I decide.

Choose one: ☐ **Harlequin Special Edition** ☐ **Harlequin Heartwarming**
(235/335 HDN GRJV) **Larger-Print**
(161/361 HDN GRJV)

Name (please print)

Address   Apt. #

City   State/Province   Zip/Postal Code

Email: Please check this box ☐ if you would like to receive newsletters and promotional emails from Harlequin Enterprises ULC and its affiliates. You can unsubscribe anytime.

Mail to the **Harlequin Reader Service:**
IN U.S.A.: P.O. Box 1341, Buffalo, NY 14240-8531
IN CANADA: P.O. Box 603, Fort Erie, Ontario L2A 5X3

Want to try 2 free books from another series? Call 1-800-873-8635 or visit www.ReaderService.com.

HSEHW22R3

HARLEQUIN
PLUS

Try the best multimedia subscription service for romance readers like you!

Read, Watch and Play.

Experience the easiest way to get the romance content you crave.

Start your **FREE TRIAL** at
www.harlequinplus.com/freetrial.